WHITE
POWER
REVE
UL WHIT'S EVE

The BOAR

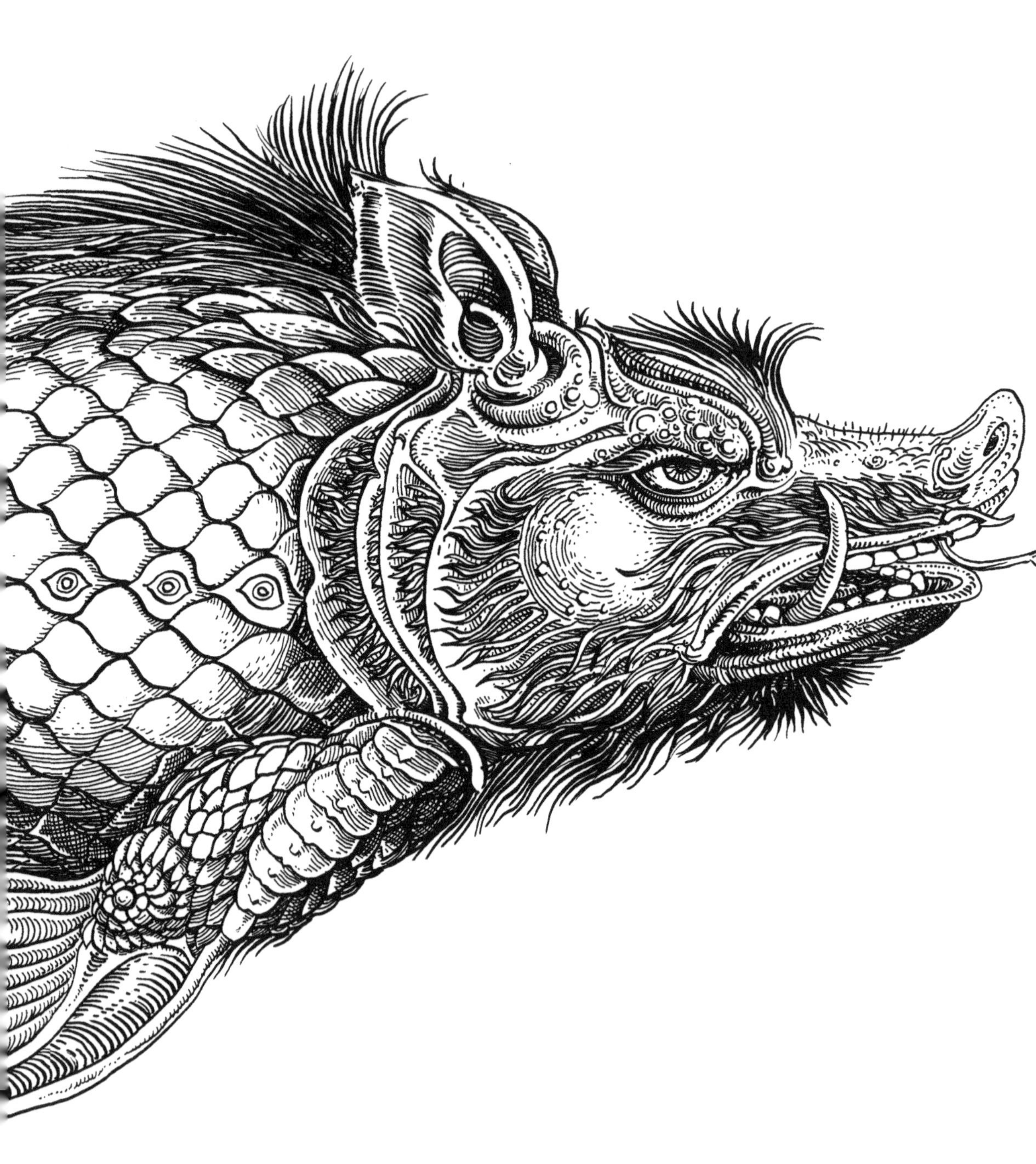

The BOAR

LEE ROY KUNZ
written by

DANIEL REED
illustrated by

LEE ROY KUNZ, MAX BARSNESS, & DANIEL REED
story by

SEPTEMTRIO
INSULA de PORCIS
OCCIDENS
ORIENS
ORIEN
Codsweep
Bulla
Tunder
ARQI
PROR
To our
Mothers
MERIDES

TABLE *of* CONTENTS

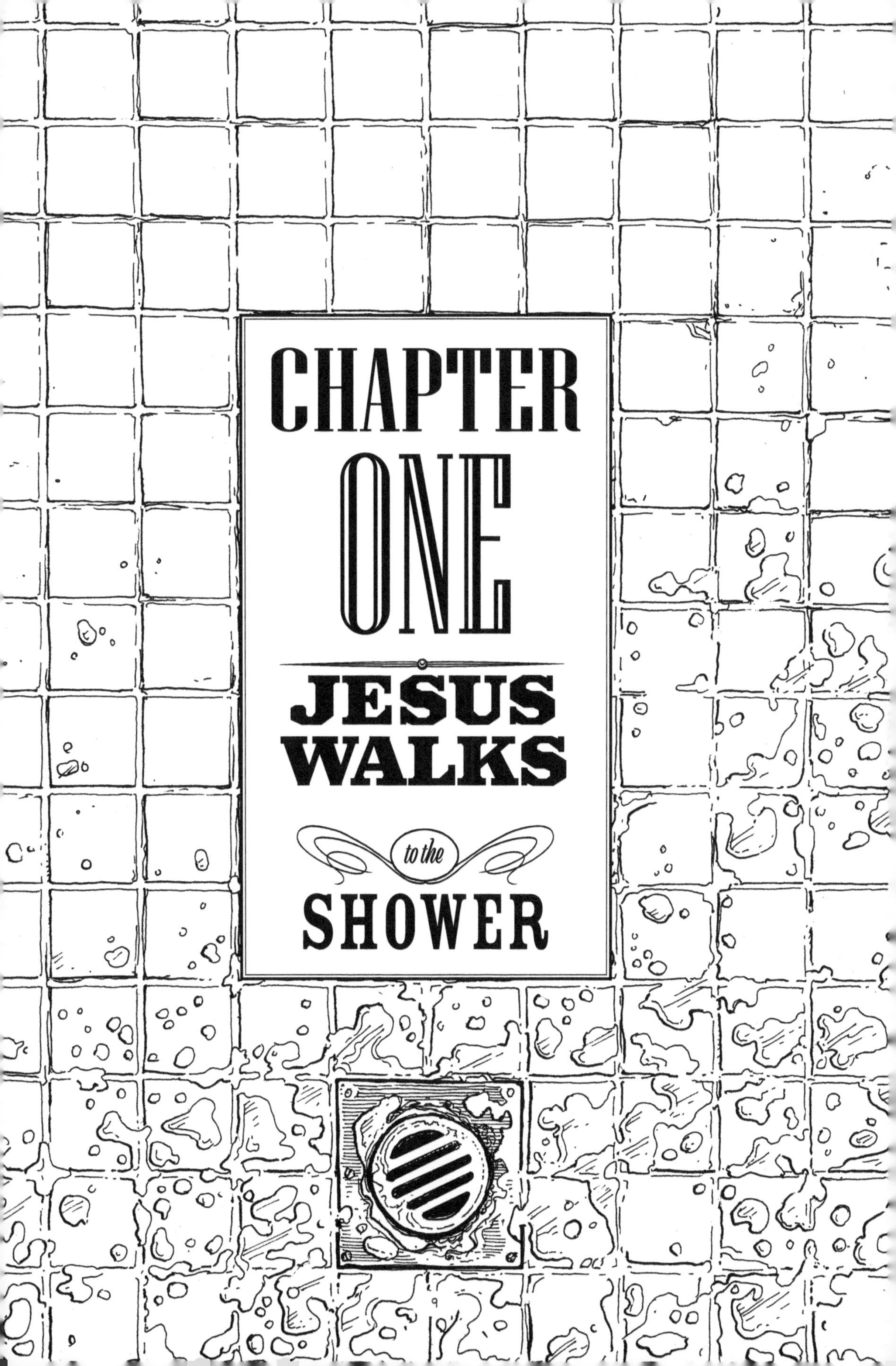
CHAPTER
ONE
JESUS WALKS
to the
SHOWER

Dear Kaia,

This will be my final letter, the last time I beg you to come visit me.

I could never hurt your Mother. I forgive her failures and love her with all my heart.

All I ask is that you sit down with me while I explain. You'll know then that what I have told you is the truth.

I am a dead man. I am being transferred from my place in solitary confinement.

Please visit me, my ladybug.

Please give me this one thing to hold on for.

I Love You,

Dad

11

AS I WALK THROUGH THE VALLEY OF THE SHADOW OF DEATH, I SHALL FEAR NO EVIL...
AL PALMER, TIME FOR YOUR TRANSFER.
KIK

DEPARTMENT OF CORRECTIONS
BLOCK B SOLITARY ROOMS 37-63
SHOWER BLOCK B
DEPARTMENT OF CORRE
KITCHEN DINING
STORE
HOLDING CELLS 4-6
GENERAL POPULATION
DEPARTMENT OF CORRECTIONS
GENERAL POPULATION

DEPARTMENT OF CORRECTIONS
DEPARTMENT OF CORRECTIONS
YOUR NEW HOME.
Aryan Brother
WHITE

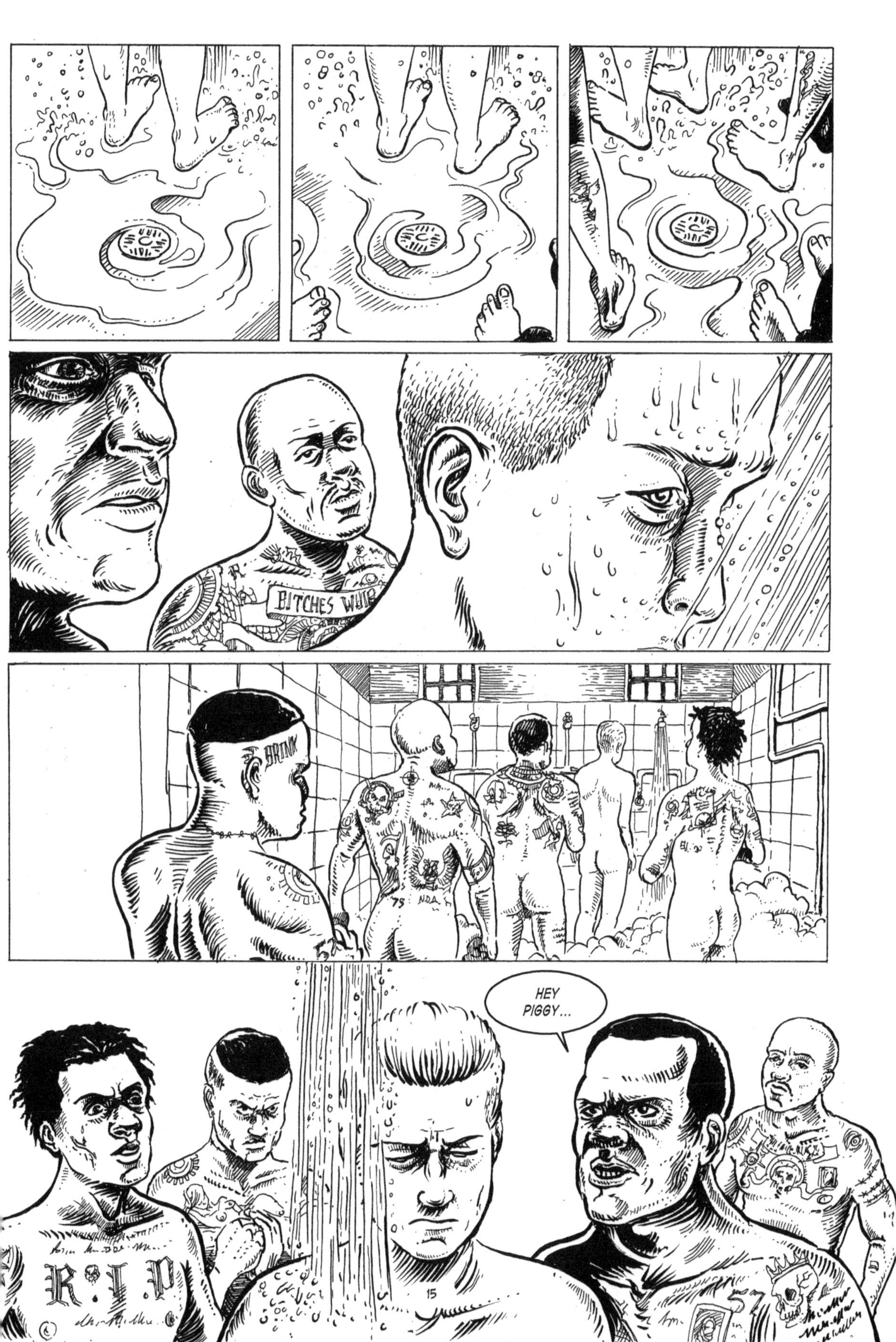
BITCHES WHIP
BRONX
R.I.P
HEY
PIGGY...
15

16

WHOOP
WHOOP WHOOP
DING DING
DING DING
ATTENTION ATTENTION! ALL PRISONERS RETURN TO YOUR CELLS

18

DING
WHOOOP
DING
WHOOP
WHOOP
DING
WHOOP
DING
WHOOOP
DING
WHOOP
WHOOP
DING
DING
WHOOP
DING
DING
BITCHE

WHAT DO YOU CRACKERS WANT?
WE AIN'T HERE TO BEEF WITH YOU, NIGGER. THE BOAR SENT US. WE'RE LOOKING FOR THE COP.
FUCK YOU, WHITE BOY!
WHOOP
DING DING
FURER
WHOOP
WHOOOOP
WHOOP
DING DING
DING
DING

WHOOOP
WHOOP
WHOOOOP
DING
DING
WHOOP
DING
DING
SOLDIER of RICH
LIONS
1949
WHITE
PRIDE

WHOOOOP DING DING
WHOOP DING WHOOOP DING
ATTENTION ATTENTION
ALL PRISONERS RETURN TO YOUR CELLS
WHOOOP DING
WHOOP DING DING

22

DEPARTMENT OF CORRECTIONS
DC SECURITY

WHOOOOP
DING
DING
DING
WHOOOP
DING
WHOOP
DING
DING
DING
WHOOP
CRACK
SNAP
SMACK

25

GASP
WHOOP
WHOOP
DEPARTMENT OF CORR
DING
DING
DING
WEAR THIS.
THEY'LL KILL YOU
IF THEY KNOW YOU'RE
A GUARD.
PARTM

26

WHOOP WHOOP
DING DING DING
YAAAH! WooHoo!
MUTHA FUCKA
WHOOP WHOOP
DING DING DING
DEPARTMENT OF CORRECTIONS
MENT CTIONS
MEN CT
ULATION
YEEHAA!!
WooHoo!
CRASH

SLUTS

WHOOP WHOOOP DING DING
WHOOP DING DING WHOOP
DEATH TO FIST
WHOOP DING DING DING DIE DIE DIE!! BURN HIM!

WHOOP WHOOP
DING
DING DING
DING DING
DING
STAND
DOWN
STAND
DOWN
DING
WHOOOP
WHOOP
DING DING
DING DING

WHOOP
ATTENTION ATTENTION ALL PRISONERS RETURN TO YOUR CELLS
DING DING DING
DING DING
WHOOP
THANK GOD! HELP ME!
WHOOP WHOOP
DING DING
NO! WAIT!
HE'S A GUARD!!! HE'S ONE OF YOU!

CRACK

WHOOP
WHOOP
DING
DING DING
DING DING
WHOOP
33

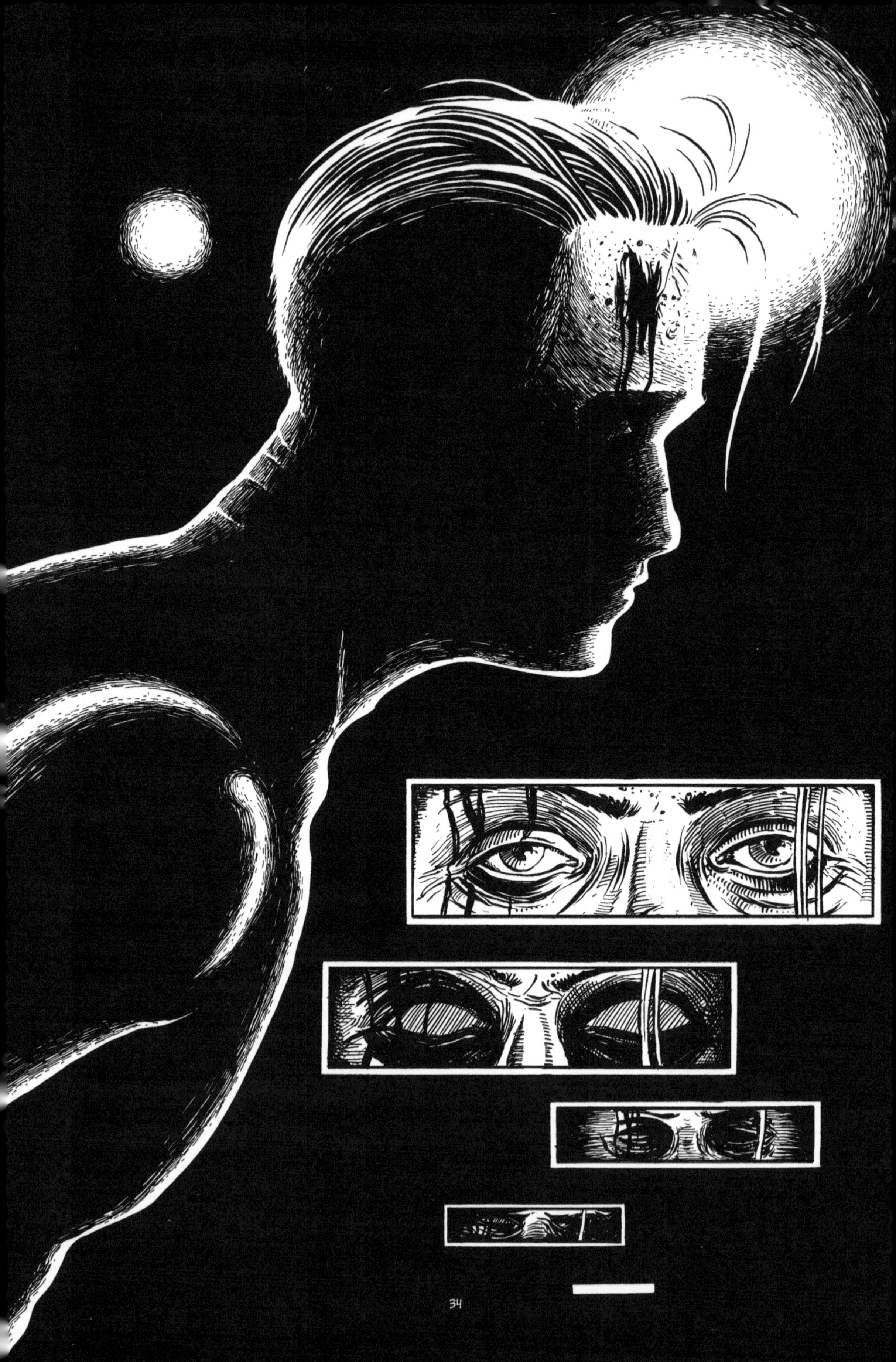

DICAL

36

...TEN YEARS EARLIER

BABE, IT'S JUST A DREAM.
YOU DON'T GET PAID ENOUGH FOR THIS.
I CAN'T STOP THINKING ABOUT BRANDON AND COLIN.
I DON'T KNOW WHY YOU STILL DO IT.
THIS ISN'T WHAT YOU SIGNED UP FOR.
SOMEONE HAS TO STOP THE BOAR... PEOPLE ARE DYING...
...FAMILIES DESTROYED.
TWO COPS HAVE ALREADY BEEN KILLED...
....WHAT ABOUT OUR FAMILY?

KAIA, DID YOU DO YOUR HOMEWORK?!
I DID!
TICKLE TICKLE
DADDY, STOP IT! *GIGGLE*

THANK YOU, NORMA.

ANYTHING FOR MY HERO.

DON'T ENCOURAGE HIM.

DADDY IS A HERO!

I'LL BE HOME LATE. I'LL TRY NOT TO WAKE YOU.

AGAIN? THIS IS EXACTLY WHAT I'M TALKING ABOUT.

I'M SORRY, I WISH IT WASN'T THIS WAY.

JUST BE CAREFUL!

I LOVE YOU.

I LOVE YOU, TOO.

THIS WILL ALL BE OVER SOON.

GRANDMA! WHERE ARE YOU GOING?!

IT WILL JUST BE A FEW DAYS. YOUR GRANDMA NEEDS TO GO TO A SPECIAL DOCTOR IN LITTLE ROCK TO TELL HER WHY HER HEAD IS SO FUZZY.

FUZZY?

FUZZY LIKE YOUR FUZZY BLANKET!

WE'RE GONNA TAKE CARE OF YOU, NORMA.
BEST CASE, IT'S ALZHEIMER'S. WORST, IT'S CANCER.
IT COULD BE NOTHING.
JUST DON'T LET ME BECOME A BURDEN. PUT ME IN A HOME IF I GET BAD.
WE WOULD NEVER DO THAT TO YOU! YOU'RE THE ROCK OF THIS FAMILY. WE WILL ALWAYS BE THERE WITH YOU.
THANK YOU, AL. YOU'RE THE BEST SON I COULD HAVE EVER ASKED FOR.

ock Station
BUT I DO THINK I AGREE WITH SARAH.
...THOSE TWO COPS YOU WORK WITH MURDERED LIKE THAT. IT'S GETTING TOO DANGEROUS. I THINK YOU SHOULD QUIT. WE MOVE TO ANOTHER TOWN.
BUT THAT'S EXACTLY WHAT THE BOAR WANTS!
I KNOW IT'S SELFISH. BUT WHY DOES IT HAVE TO BE YOU THAT SAVES THE WORLD?

PLATFORM ONE
WE'LL TALK ABOUT IT WHEN YOU GET BACK.

I THINK I'M BEING FOLLOWED. CAN YOU RUN A PLATE?

CAN YOU REPEAT THAT, AL?
FALSE ALARM.
THEY DROVE ON.
I'M GETTING PARANOID.
TE POL
CALLING ALL UNITS.
CALLING ALL UNITS.
MULTIPLE HOMICIDES AT THE METAL YARD... 653 COTTON.
45

STATE POLICE
720B
MARSHALL, WHAT IS IT?
IT'S OFFICER JIMENIZ. TRUST ME, PALMER. YOU DON'T WANT TO SEE WHAT THEY DID TO HER.
46

THE BOAR IS
INSIDE YOU
47

BOAR IS
SIDE YOU

CHIEF WHITE?

LET'S GET OUT OF HERE, PALMER. THE FBI IS GONNA TAKE OVER FROM HERE.
THE FBI?! SHE'S ONE OF OURS! WE CAN'T JUST STEP ASIDE.

THEY'RE TAKING OVER THE INVESTIGATION. ANYTHING RELATED TO THE BOAR GOES TO THEM NOW.

BUT SIR, I THINK I MIGHT HAVE FINALLY FIGURED OUT WHO THE BOAR IS.

HALF MY OFFICERS HAVE ALREADY QUIT OR BEEN KILLED. THE OTHER HALF ARE SCARED FOR THEIR LIVES.

JUST LET ME EXPLAIN.
...IT ALL CONNECTS TO LT. GOVERNOR JIM PICKETT.
...OWNER OF HEAVENLY FARMS.
OPIUM from Afganastan
ARKANSAS Politics
PIG
SHRIMP BOATS
THE BOAR
3 DEAD
GULF SHIPPING BOATS
PINK GOAT
HE HAS LINKS TO VIOLENT WHITE SUPREMACIST GROUPS. I BELIEVE HE IS USING THEM TO CARRY OUT THESE MURDERS TO SCARE US AND MAKE US THINK IT'S THE CARTEL.
BUT I NEED TO FOLLOW UP A LEAD IN HOT SPRINGS.
49

THIS IS GOOD WORK, PALMER. BUT YOU SHOULD TURN WHATEVER YOU HAVE OVER TO THE FEDS.
I CAN'T!
... HE'S KILLED PEOPLE WE KNOW AND LOVE. THIS IS PERSONAL NOW.
I'M SORRY, AL. BUT THIS IS A WAR.
WE'RE NOT EQUIPPED TO TAKE ON THIS KIND OF VIOLENCE ALONE. WE NEED THE FEDS.
BUT SIR...
IT'S TIME TO BE DONE WITH THIS.
I HATE THE FEDS AS MUCH AS YOU DO. BUT THEY WILL TAKE IT FROM HERE.
THE BOAR IS THEIR PROBLEM NOW.

LATER THAT NIGHT...
DADDY!
KAIA, WHAT'S WRONG?
I HEARD FIREWORKS!
FIREWORKS?

I CALLED FOR MOMMY! BUT SHE DIDN'T ANSWER.

IT'S OKAY. MY LITTLE PRINCESS.

GO BACK TO SLEEP. I LOVE YOU.

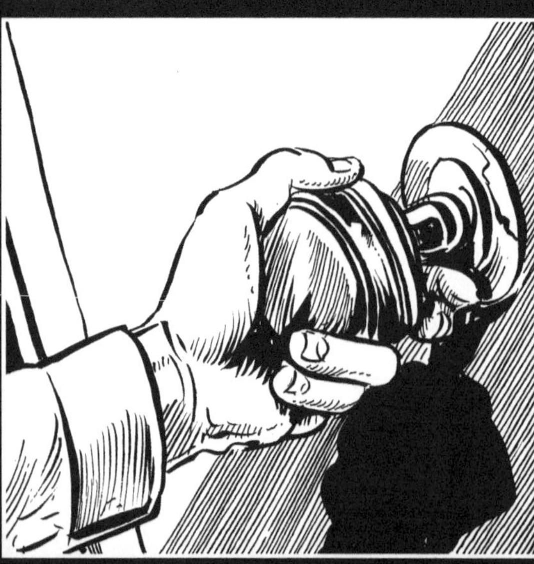

OH, GOD! NO!!! SARAH!

53

SARAH!
MY ANGEL!

YOU WERE
CHEATING ON ME?

AL PALMER, YOU HAVE BEEN FOUND GUILTY ON TWO COUNTS OF FIRST-DEGREE MURDER.
I HEREBY SENTENCE YOU TO... TWO CONSECUTIVE LIFE SENTENCES. ONE FOR EACH OF YOUR VICTIMS.
KAIA!
KAIA!
...YOUR RECKLESS ACCUSATIONS AGAINST JIM PICKETT, A RESPECTED BUSINESS LEADER, ARE PREPOSTEROUS AND SELF-SERVING!
WHITE COP KILLS BLACK WIFE
WSJ OPINION: THE CONVICTION OF OFFICER AL PALMER...FOUND GUILTY IN THE COURT OF PUBLIC OPINION...IT SEEMS THE TRUTH NO LONGER MATTERS.
CORRECTION
SLAM

DADDY!!!
I MISS YOU.

KAIA?
PLEASE,
TALK TO ME.

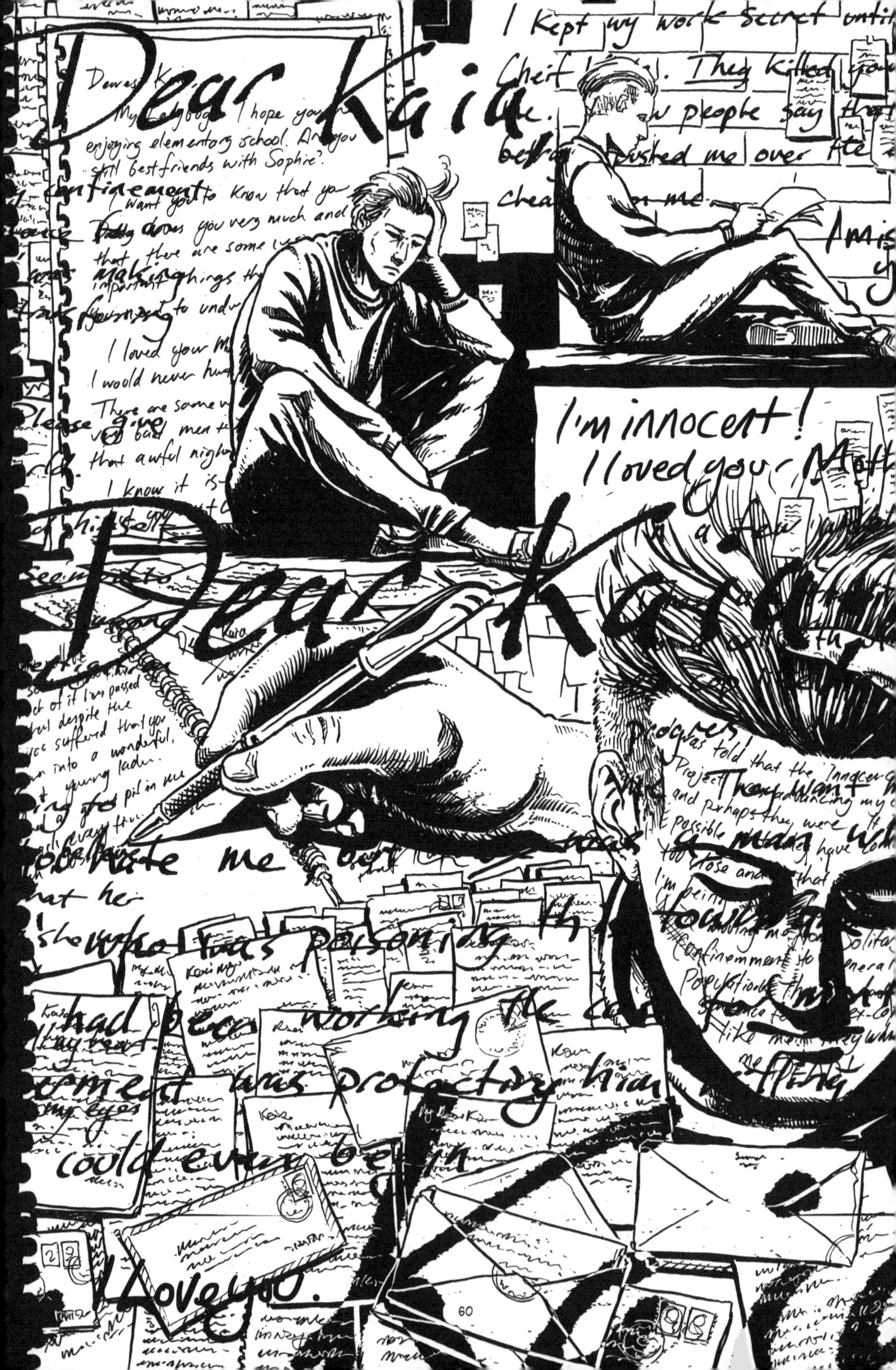
Dear Kaia
Dear Kaia
I'm innocent!
I loved your Mom
I love you.
60

CHAPTER TWO
Freedom

Dear Kaia,

They expect me to believe it was a computer glitch that resulted in my transfer. I will be placed back in Solitary when I am released from the hospital, but I think someone is trying to have me killed.

My lawyer Sam tells me the 'Innocence Project' is dedicating more resources to my case. They might have found something.

If you won't talk to me, talk to him.

I love you,

Dad.

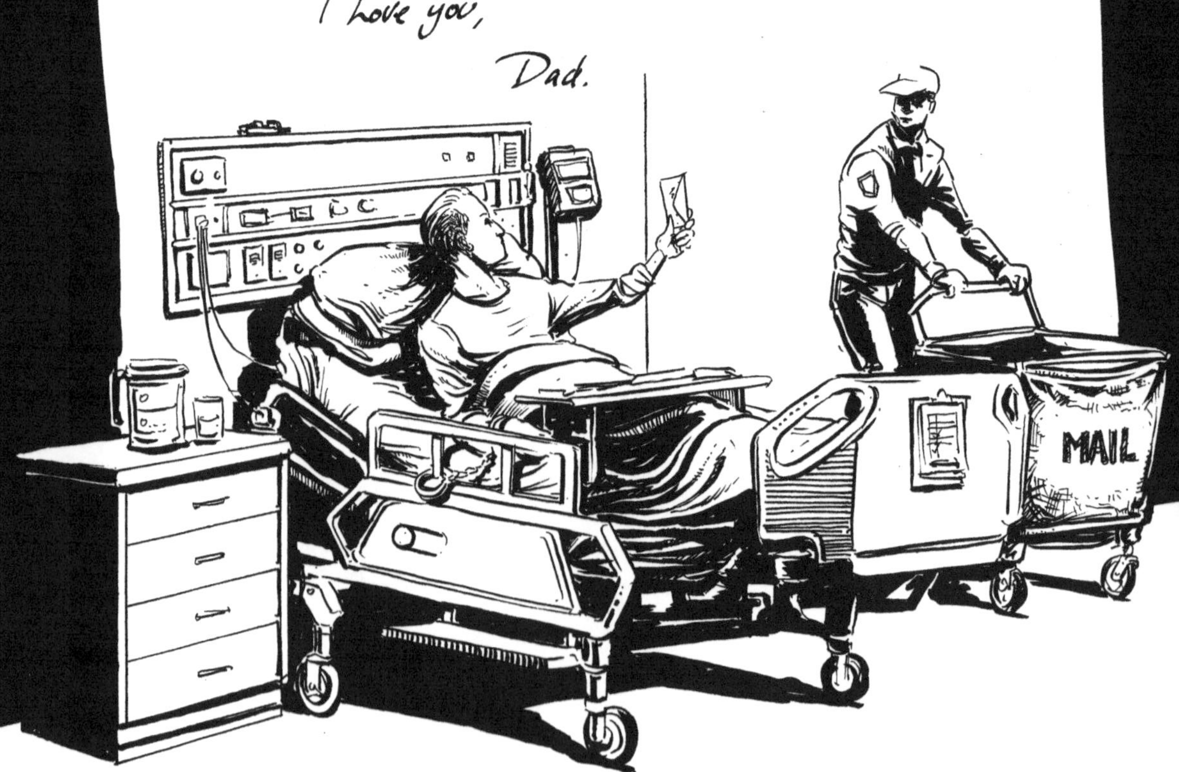

PRESENT DAY...
HE'S MY FATHER.
HE'S A WHITE CIS-GENDER CONSERVATIVE.
BUT MAYBE HE DIDN'T DO IT?
HE'S A COP. HE'S GUILTY ENOUGH.
HAVEN'T YOU HEARD OF THE "BLUE WALL OF SILENCE?"
THEY'RE ALL IN IT TOGETHER.
I'M SORRY, SIR, THIS CARD HAS ALSO BEEN DECLINED.
DADDY! ALL MY FRIENDS ARE COMING OVER!
I'M SORRY SWEETHEART.
WE'LL HAVE TO FIGURE SOMETHING ELSE OUT.
HERE. LET ME.
WHAT?!

IT'S TEN DOLLARS. JUST PAY IT FORWARD.
MISS, THANK YOU...

DON'T WORRY ABOUT IT. WE'VE ALL BEEN THERE.
Flour
Sugar
king
Cracker
Crisps
Cookies

YOU DON'T KNOW WHAT THIS MEANS TO US. THANK YOU, YOUNG LADY! GOD BLESS.

WHY WOULD YOU HELP THOSE PEOPLE?
HE EVEN MISGENDERED YOU!

IT WAS TEN DOLLARS.

...YOU SEE HIS LITTLE GIRL?
KARENS HAVE TO START SOMEWHERE.

MEANWHILE...
BLOCK B
ROOMS

THIS IS FROM ME AND THE OTHER GUARDS.

WE SAW THE SECURITY FOOTAGE. HOW YOU TRIED TO HELP ELIJAH.
IS HE GONNA BE OKAY?
DEPA
OF COR
LEAVES BEHIND A WIFE AND THREE KIDS. THE FUCKING ANIMALS.

GOD, I'M SORRY... HIS POOR FAMILY.

WE SAVED A NUMBER IN THERE FOR YOU.

...YOUR DAUGHTER, KAIA.

REYNAULDS ST
DEFUND the POLICE
STOP
NO JUSTICE.
NO PEACE.
ABOLISH THE POLICE.
WHITE SHAME
DEPARTMENT CORRECTIONS
EP
FT

66

HANDS UP!
DON'T SHOOT!
WHITE PRIVILEGE!
END RACISM NOW
RING RING
HELLO?
WHO IS THIS?
KAIA?

KAIA...
...DON'T HANG UP... PLEASE JUST LISTEN.

.....
KAIA...?

HOW DID YOU GET THIS NUMBER?
FIGHT
TH
POW

HAVE YOU GOT MY LETTERS?

YES. PLEASE, STOP SENDING THEM!

MY LAWYER, SAM, AT THE INNOCENCE PROJECT...

...HAS HE TALKED TO YOU? HE SAID YOU COULD HELP.

I TOLD HIM... I DON'T KNOW...NOT UNTIL HE HAS PROOF.

I HAVE TO GO.

CALL ENDED

DEFUND THE POLICE!

NO JUSTICE!
NO PEACE!

70

ONE MONTH LATER...
RECEPTION

BLOCK B
SOLITARY
ROOMS

LEO TOLSTOY
THE KINGDOM of GOD is WITHIN YOU

OFFICER PALMER...

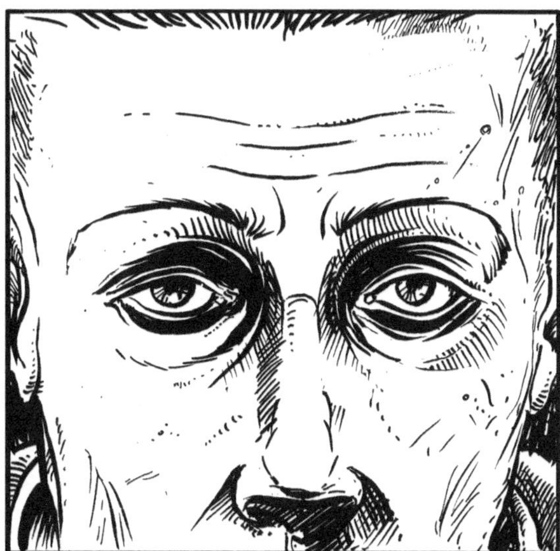

MY GOD, HAS IT REALLY BEEN TEN YEARS?

CHIEF WHITE?

HAVE YOU HEARD FROM YOUR LAWYER, SAM?

I AM SORRY.

I'M SO SORRY....

I DON'T KNOW HOW TO SAY THIS...

THAT SUPPOSED 'COMPUTER GLITCH' THAT LED TO YOUR TRANSFER....
IT PROVED SOMEONE WANTS YOU DEAD. THEY WERE ABLE TO REOPEN YOUR CASE AND...

YOU'RE BEING RELEASED.

I ALWAYS KNEW YOU WERE INNOCENT.

DOES MY DAUGHTER KNOW?

I WANT TO TALK TO KAIA.

CHIEF?! MY DAUGHTER?!
I'VE BEEN TRYING TO GET A HOLD OF HER.

BUT YOU HAVE TO UNDERSTAND...
...WE DID EVERYTHING WE COULD TO PROTECT YOU.

... BUT YOU WERE COVERED IN HER BLOOD.

YOU SHOWERED.
WHY DID YOU SHOWER?
IT MADE YOU LOOK GUILTY.
I KNOW YOU WERE IN SHOCK...BUT...
I'M SORRY AL.

I HAVE TWO OFFICERS UNDERCOVER RIGHT NOW WITH THE WHITE LIONS.
THE WHITE SUPREMACIST GROUP THAT HAD ORDERS TO KILL YOU FROM THE BOAR.
THEY DON'T WANT YOU GETTING OUT... ...THEY'RE SCARED OF YOU, AL...

HOW WOULD YOU LIKE TO BE A COP AGAIN?

...TO FINISH THE INVESTIGATION YOU STARTED? NOBODY KNOWS THE BOAR INVESTIGATION BETTER THAN YOU.

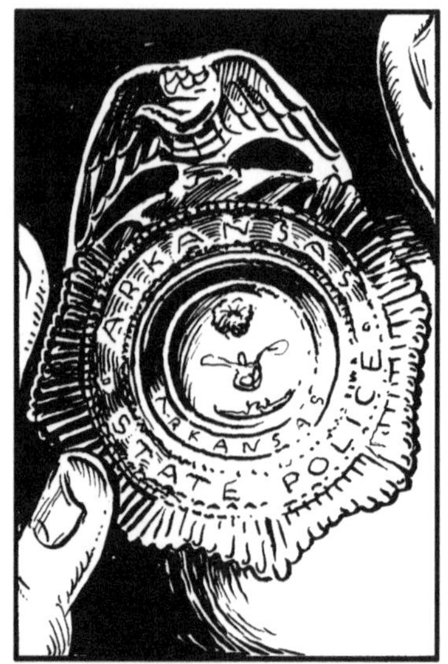

ARE YOU SERIOUS?!

THOSE MEN KILLED YOUR WIFE.

I WANT TO SEE KAIA.
I'VE GOT MY BEST MEN LOOKING FOR HER...AND SHE GOES BY 'SEVEN' NOW.

WHOOP WHOOP
CRAP!

YOU KAIA PALMER?
MY NAME IS SEVEN.

RIGHT. I'M DETECTIVE BYRON. THAT'S DETECTIVE COLBA.

WHAT DO YOU FASCISTS WANT?

CHIEF WHITE ASKED US TO BRING YOU INTO THE STATION. HE HAS IMPORTANT NEWS ABOUT YOUR FATHER.
AM I BEING ARRESTED?
NO, MISS.
THEN TELL GEORGE TO GO FUCK HIMSELF!
AM I GETTING OLD?...OR IS THERE SOMETHING SERIOUSLY WRONG WITH THIS GENERATION?
CHIEF WHITE CAN GO FUCK HIMSELF.

LATER THAT NIGHT...
PINK COAT
COLBA, YOU GOOD?
WE'RE SUPPOSED TO BE UNDERCOVER AND HE'S SENDING US OUT LIKE ERRAND BOYS...IT'S LIKE CHIEF WHITE IS TRYING TO GET US KILLED.
NEVER ASCRIBE TO MALICE THAT WHICH CAN EASILY BE EXPLAINED BY STUPIDITY.
STAFF ONLY

SNIFF,
GREAT.

PAYMENT
COMPLETE.

WHERE Y'ALL
THINK YOU'RE
HEADED?

THE PARTY
JUST STARTED.

GENTLEMEN, THIS IS ALEXIS.

SHE'S THIRTEEN.

SHE LOOKS A BIT YOUNG.
WE'RE NOT DOING THAT.
YOU WANT TO MEET THE BOAR?
GET UP.

NO FUCKING WAY!

THIS IS HOW IT WORKS HERE...

...YOU PROVE TO US YOU'RE NOT A COP.

FINE. THEN I GUESS WE'RE COPS.
THAT A THREAT?

EVERYONE PUT YOUR GUNS AWAY!
YOU WANT PROOF?

LET'S GO.

VIP
SUITE

SHOULD I READ YOU YOUR RIGHTS NOW OR LATER?
FUCK YOU. I JUST SAVED OUR LIVES.
HEY!
COME BY THE CLUBHOUSE NEXT WEEK...
NOW, THAT WE KNOW WE CAN TRUST AT LEAST ONE OF YOU.
...IT'S TIME Y'ALL MET THE THE BOAR. GET SOME FACE TIME. TAKE THIS RELATIONSHIP TO THE NEXT LEVEL.
YES, SIR.
HAHAHA! YOU HEAR THAT? "THE BOAR!"

THE NEXT MORNING...

WHAT HAPPENED TO MY BREAKFAST?
YOU DON'T REMEMBER, NANA?
YOU ATE IT ALREADY.
NO, I DIDN'T!
WHY ARE YOU LYING TO ME?
DING DONG

CHIEF WHITE? WHAT THE FUCK DOES HE WANT?!
WILL YOU STOP HARRASING ME!
WHEN'S THE LAST TIME YOU SAW YOUR FATHER?

90

MURDERER!
KAIA, IT'S ME. YOUR DADDY.
I CAME AND TUCKED YOU IN THAT NIGHT.
REMEMBER???

YOU'RE NOT MY DAD...

...YOU'RE JUST THE WHITE MAN WHO KILLED MY MOTHER!

92

MASC
MASSES
emancipation
Absolute right of the
Freedom of cons
IS A BRICK
It's my view
that gender is
culturally formed
but it's also a
domain of agency
freedom an
that it is mostly
to do with govern
important
posed by idea
norm
again
who a
differ
93

THE NEXT DAY...
ZODIAC
GASP!
CARL MARX DAS KAPITAL
FOUCAULT POWER/KNOWLEDGE
UNDOING GENDER
JUDITH BUTLER
RADICALISM
LEFT of MA
CRY UNITY
FREEDOM DREAM
BLACK LEFT
LUMUMBA
GILES DELUEZE
ANTI-OEDIPUS
PIERE BOURDIEU
MASCULINE DOMINATION
STRUGGLE
Revolution
RADICAL
BLACK BOLSHEVIK
People TRIUMPH
HAMMER & HELL
BLACK MARX
BLACK... RED
CUBAS RACIAL CO.
COMMUNISTS N HARLEM
CASE for FREEDOM
SEXUAL
CAR
K
94

AFRICAN AMERICAN RADICA
LEFT
SOCIA
THE
FEMA

OH GOD, DAD.
WHAT HAVE I DONE?!

I still love he
I love you. I wi
I am innocent.
I forgive you fo
me, for wishing I w
Nothing could eve
I love you Kaia.
You are my daughter.
Love, Dad.

98

99

FLOOR
Sniff
Sniff
WHEEZE

COUGH
HACK
NANA!
COUGH
WHEEZE
I'M SUPPOSED
TO PICK UP MY DAD
IN AN HOUR!
I DON'T HAVE
TIME TO TAKE
YOU TO THE E.R.!
HE'S ALREADY
GONNA HATE ME!

STOP
DEPARTMENT OF CORRECTIONS
STOP

HEY! YOU AL PALMER?
HOP IN, BROTHER!
I'M ACTUALLY WAITING FOR MY DAUGHTER.
KAIA, RIGHT? SHE ORDERED YOU AN UBER. IT'S LIKE A TAXI...

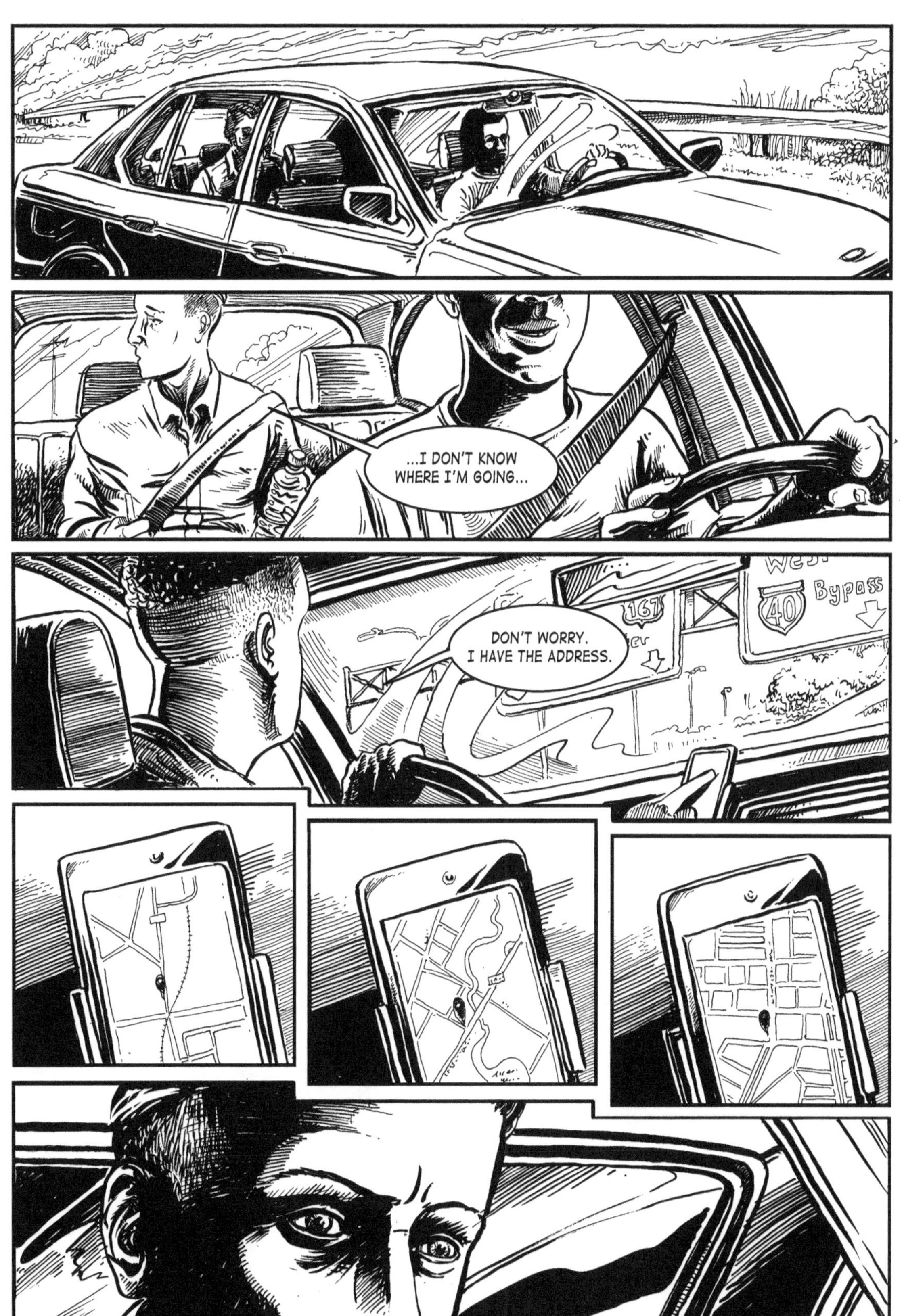

...I DON'T KNOW WHERE I'M GOING...
DON'T WORRY. I HAVE THE ADDRESS.

Cafe
BOB'S BIKES

ΑΣ
KEEP HATE off CAMPUS
BAN HATE SPEECH

WHAT HAPPENED TO THIS PLACE?

HAVE A GOOD DAY, SIR. PLEASE ASK KAIA TO GIVE ME FIVE STARS.
I WILL. THANK YOU.

108

ZZZZ...
SARAH?

YOU DON'T FIND MUCH FISH OUT HERE NOW-A-DAYS.
IS THIS HEAVEN?
IF THIS WAS HEAVEN, YOU'D THINK THERE'D BE BETTER FISHING.
He He He

114

DON'T CLOSE YOUR EYES, SON. *OPEN THEM.*

THE MONSTERS
ARE STILL
OUT THERE.

VROOOM
SLAM

OH, MY GOD!
HE ESCAPED!

NANA, REMEMBER WHAT WE TALKED ABOUT? DAD IS INNOCENT.
BUT... YOU SAID?!
DAD'S BACK NOW. IT'S OKAY. HE DIDN'T KILL MOM.

I...I'M CALLING THE POLICE.
I'M SO SORRY, DAD! WILL YOU PLEASE FORGIVE ME?!
OF COURSE, HONEY...
YOU'LL ALWAYS BE MY LITTLE GIRL.
I'M NOT REALLY A GIRL ANYMORE....
YOU KNOW WHAT... WE'LL TALK ABOUT THAT LATER. I'M JUST HAPPY YOU'RE BACK!

NORMA, IT'S ME. REMEMBER? YOUR SON-IN-LAW, AL.
GET AWAY FROM ME!
cheetos
MURDERER!
HOW BAD IS IT?
GOOD DAYS AND BAD... IT'S NOT COMPLETELY DEGENERATIVE. SHE CAN STILL LEARN SOME NEW THINGS...
GIVE HER TIME.
SHE'S CALLING THE COPS.
DON'T WORRY. THAT HASN'T BEEN CONNECTED FOR YEARS.

YOU'LL NEED THAT NOW THAT YOU'RE OUT.
THANK YOU!
AL? IS THAT REALLY YOU?
SEE, SHE'S ALREADY STARTING TO REMEMBER.
HI, NORMA! I MISSED YOU!
LOOK, THERE IS FACETIME, MAPS, MUSIC...
122

THIS IS SO SWEET! THANK YOU, PRINCESS!
YOU'RE WELCOME!
TRY FACE-TIMING ME! I'M IN YOUR FAVORITES!
Seven

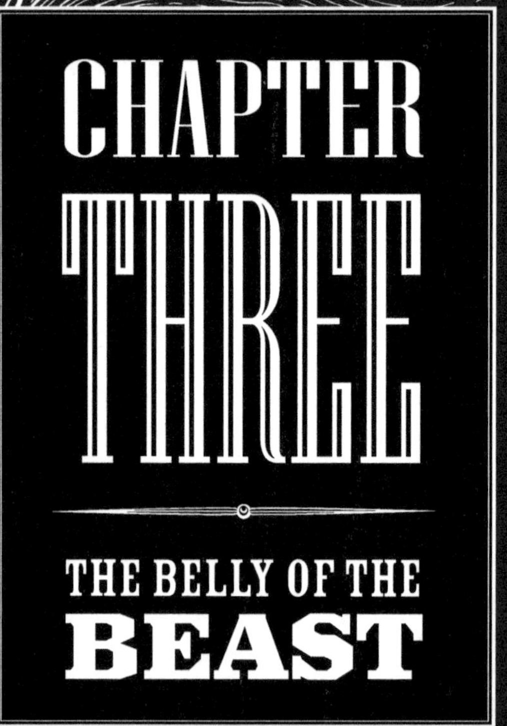

Dear Kaia,

I only wish to give you back the years you have lost.
The time with a father that was taken from you.
There is so little justice in this world.

Jim Picket is THE BOAR. He murdered your mother and
framed me... our government is evil. Our politicians corrupt.
Don't ever trust them, as I so foolishly did.

Stupidity is more dangerous than evil.

I Love You,
Dad.

Heavenly
Farms

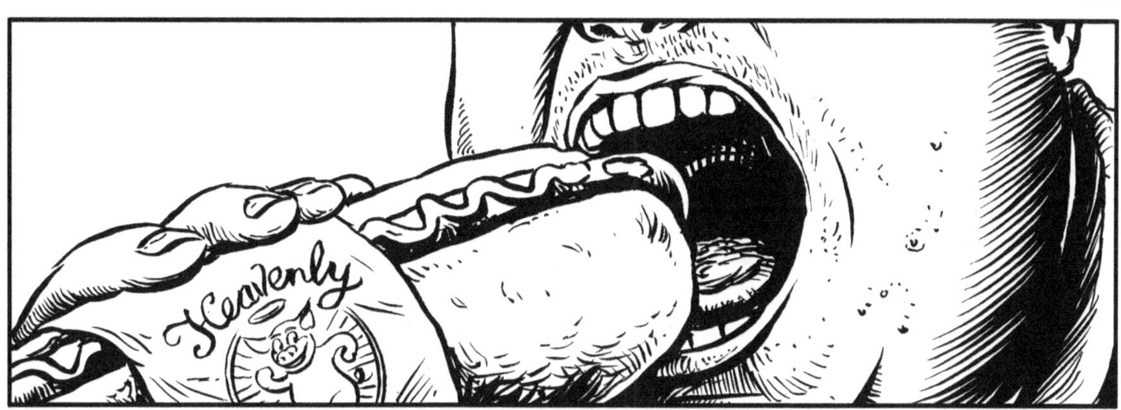

Heavenly

JIM PICKET for GOVERNOR
Heavenly Farms
JIM PICKET GOVERNOR
JIM PICKET
Heavenly Farms
JIM PICKET for GOVERNOR
Heavenly Farms

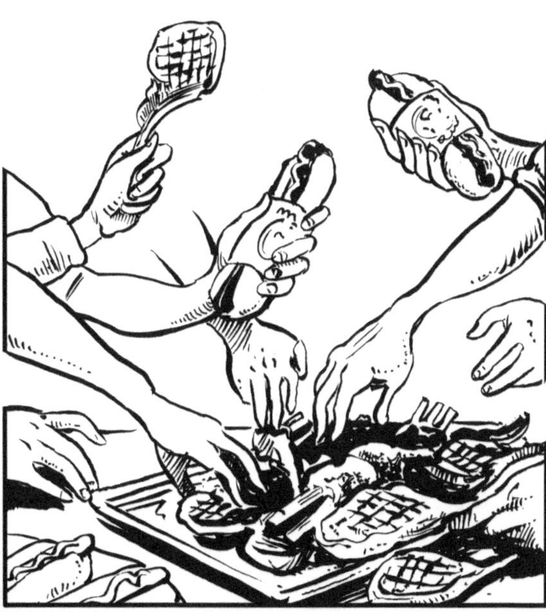

GOD BLESS YOU ALL, FOR STANDING WITH ME AGAINST THIS LIBERAL WITCH-HUNT!

CAN YOU GUYS HEAR US?
LOUD AND CLEAR.
YOU SHOULDN'T BE WEARING A WIRE.
IT'S TOO SOON!
YOU REALLY WANT TO RISK DYING FOR THIS?
...MY GRANDMOTHER ESCAPED THE POLISH GHETTO.
I KNOW! I KNOW! WILL YOU PLEASE SHUT THE FUCK UP ABOUT IT.
EXIT
NEVER STOP THE FIGHT

LOOK WHAT THE CAT DRAGGED IN.

GOOD TO SEE Y'ALL. WHERE'S EVERYBODY HEADED?

YOU'RE GONNA STAY HERE AND MEET THE BOSS.

YOU COME WITH US...
WE'RE GONNA GO FOR SOME GAMBLING...

HE SAYS HE CAN'T TRUST YOU YET. SO THE BOAR AND YOUR FRIEND ARE GOING TO GET ACQUAINTED INSTEAD...

WHITE

SHIT! THE'VE SEPERATED THEM.
WHO DO WE FOLLOW?
DO WE STAY WITH COLBA OR GO WITH BYRON?
WHAT DO WE DO CHIEF?
BYRON IS THE ONE WITH THE WIRE. WE GO WITH HIM.
WHAT ABOUT COLBA?
HE'S GOING TO HAVE TO LOOK AFTER HIMSELF. BYRON HAS THE WIRE...
AND WE'RE ABOUT TO LOSE SIGNAL.
MOVE, MOVE, MOVE!
POLICE
POLICE
POLICE

I HAVE A DREAM....
...THAT ONE DAY ALL AMERICANS WILL BE AS RICH AS ME.

THIS COUNTRY IS A BUSINESS.

IT SHOULD BE RUN LIKE ONE.

I AM JIM PICKET. AND A VOTE FOR ME, IS A VOTE FOR FOUR MORE YEARS OF MAKING THIS STATE GREAT AGAIN!

SQUEEEEEE
135

WE JUST FED
"OFFICER COLBA"
TO THE PIGGIES.

AND WE TOOK BYRON TO THE CASINO LIKE YOU ASKED.
WHAT DO YOU WANT US TO DO WITH HIM THERE?
SQUEEEE
WHITE

137

SQUEEEE
Heavenly Farms
Heavenly Farms
Heavenly Farms

MEANWHILE...

JACKPOT

JACK AND COKE, PLEASE.

$5
THIS ONE IS ON ME, HANDSOME.

HOW MUCH LONGER UNTIL I CAN SEE MY PARTNER?
LET'S FINISH THIS POT.
EXIT

$5
CALL.

NOW, I WANT TO SEE MY PARTNER!
YOU SNEAKY LITTLE JEW...
WHAT DID YOU CALL ME?
THERE BUT FOR THE GRACE OF GOD... YOU'RE ONE LUCKY KIKE...
YOU GUYS HEAR THAT? WE HAVE A PROBLEM.

OINK. OINK.

BONANZA
JACKPOT
Royal
FLUSH
$
$
145

THE BOAR

WOW, MISTER. ARE YOU OKAY?

THIS IS OFFICER BYRON! I'VE BEEN DRUGGED! OFFICER DOWN!

OH, MY GOD.
ARE THOSE TEETH?
BONUS
FREE SPIN

OCT 24·2019
01:38PM
SWAT! MOVE! MOVE!
DOES ANYONE HAVE EYES ON, COLBA?!
LAST WE SAW, HE WAS STILL AT THE CLUBHOUSE.

STAND DOWN! I REPEAT! CHIEF WHITE SAYS STAND DOWN!
POLICE
DEA

FUCK THIS! I'M GOING IN!
DEA

150

SWAT
SWAT
SW

CHIEF WHITE?

OCT 24·2019
04 38 PM

THIS WAS
A SETUP.

EA
POLICE
DEA

RIVER
A3
POLICE
STATE TROOPER

THE LADY THAT GAVE ME THE BOX SAID IT WAS JUST A JOKE.
OFFICER BYRON....
CHIEF?

DENTAL CAME BACK. I'M VERY SORRY. IT WAS OFFICER COLBA.
WE RAIDED THE CLUB HOUSE, BUT THEY WERE ALREADY GONE.

...I KNOW YOU WERE VERY CLOSE.
HOW DID THEY KNOW?!

I PROMISE YOU, BYRON.
POLICE LINE DO NOT CROSS

THE BOAR WON'T GET AWAY WITH THIS.

THE NEXT MORNING...
KNOCK
KNOCK

CHIEF, WHAT IS ALL THIS?
CAN WE TALK IN PRIVATE?

MY DAUGHTER CAN HEAR WHAT YOU HAVE TO SAY.
THIS IS ALL EVIDENCE WE HAVE COLLECTED OVER THE YEARS ON THE BOAR. INCLUDING YOUR WIFE'S MURDER.
CASE FILE J-P
CASE FILE Q-Z

I WAS HOPING IT MIGHT HELP YOU RECONSIDER MY OFFER.
TO BE A COP AGAIN?
FUCK THAT!

TO HELP US FINALLY BREAK THIS CASE. GET JUSTICE.
IS THIS EVEN LEGAL?

MOST OF THIS EVIDENCE WAS SQUASHED BY THE PROSECUTION.
SUE THE D.A. NOT THE DEPARTMENT.

THAT'S WHAT THIS IS ABOUT? TO KEEP ME FROM SUING YOU?!

...BUT I FEEL LIKE IT'S MY ONLY CHOICE...
JIM PICKET HAS ONLY GOTTEN MORE POWERFUL SINCE YOU'VE BEEN AWAY. HE'S THE GOVERNOR, NOW UP FOR RE-ELECTION!
YOU SUE US, IT WILL DESTROY ANY INVESTIGATION WE DO HAVE. I JUST LOST ANOTHER ONE OF MY OFFICERS. WE'RE SO CLOSE!
I WANT YOU TO PLEASE LEAVE.
I'M RISKING MY CAREER BRINGING YOU THIS.

PLEASE, LEAVE. AND TAKE THIS WITH YOU.

TAKE A LOOK AT IT, PLEASE.

I KNOW OFFICER PALMER IS STILL IN THERE SOMEWHERE.

CASE FILE A-K

LATER THAT WEEK...

I WANT TO
SEE DADDY.

OFFICER BYRON... CAN I HAVE A WORD WITH YOU?

WHAT DO YOU WANT, CHIEF?

I THINK YOU SHOULD TAKE SOME TIME OFF.

THAT'S NOT GONNA HAPPEN. I'M GONNA FIND THE MEN THAT DID THIS.

COLBA DID IT TO HIMSELF.

TAKE A LOOK AT THIS BANK STATEMENT.

I DON'T BELIEVE IT.
OFFICER COLBA, HAD AN ACCOUNT WITH OVER TWELVE MILLION DOLLARS IN IT.
SMALL DEPOSITS MADE OVER THE LAST TEN YEARS.
HE WAS ONE OF THEM.
THIS IS FUCKING BULLSHIT!
I KNOW COLBA WAS A SCUMBAG. BUT HE WASN'T DIRTY LIKE THIS! THIS IS ANOTHER FRAMEJOB.

WHY DO YOU THINK THEY KILLED HIM AND NOT YOU? ...

LUCK. THAT COUNTS FOR MORE IN THIS LIFE THAN...

THEY EVEN KNEW YOU WERE JEWISH!

IF WE SHOULD BE LOOKING AT ANYBODY, IT'S YOU.

YOU'RE GRIEVING. I'M GONNA TRY AND NOT TAKE THAT PERSONALLY.

AS YOU WISH, SIR.

TAKE SOME TIME OFF, BYRON!

BYRON!

WHOEVER THE BOAR IS, I'M GONNA FIND HIM AND I'M GONNA KILL HIM.

BYRON!

BYRON!

A DECORATED EUREKA SPRINGS COUNTY POLICE DETECTIVE WAS KILLED LAST WEEK WHILE UNDERCOVER WITH A VIOLENT WHITE SUPREMACIST GROUP...
OFFICER COLBA WAS A HIGHLY DECORATED WAR VETERAN, COMPLETING THREE TOURS OF AFGHANISTAN.
A STRONG DESIRE TO FURTHER SERVE HIS COMMUNITY LED HIM TO JOIN THE POLICE FORCE UPON HIS RETURN, THIS TIME TO FIGHT THE WAR ON DRUGS...
NBC
BREAKING: AMERICAN HERO LAID TO REST
NBC

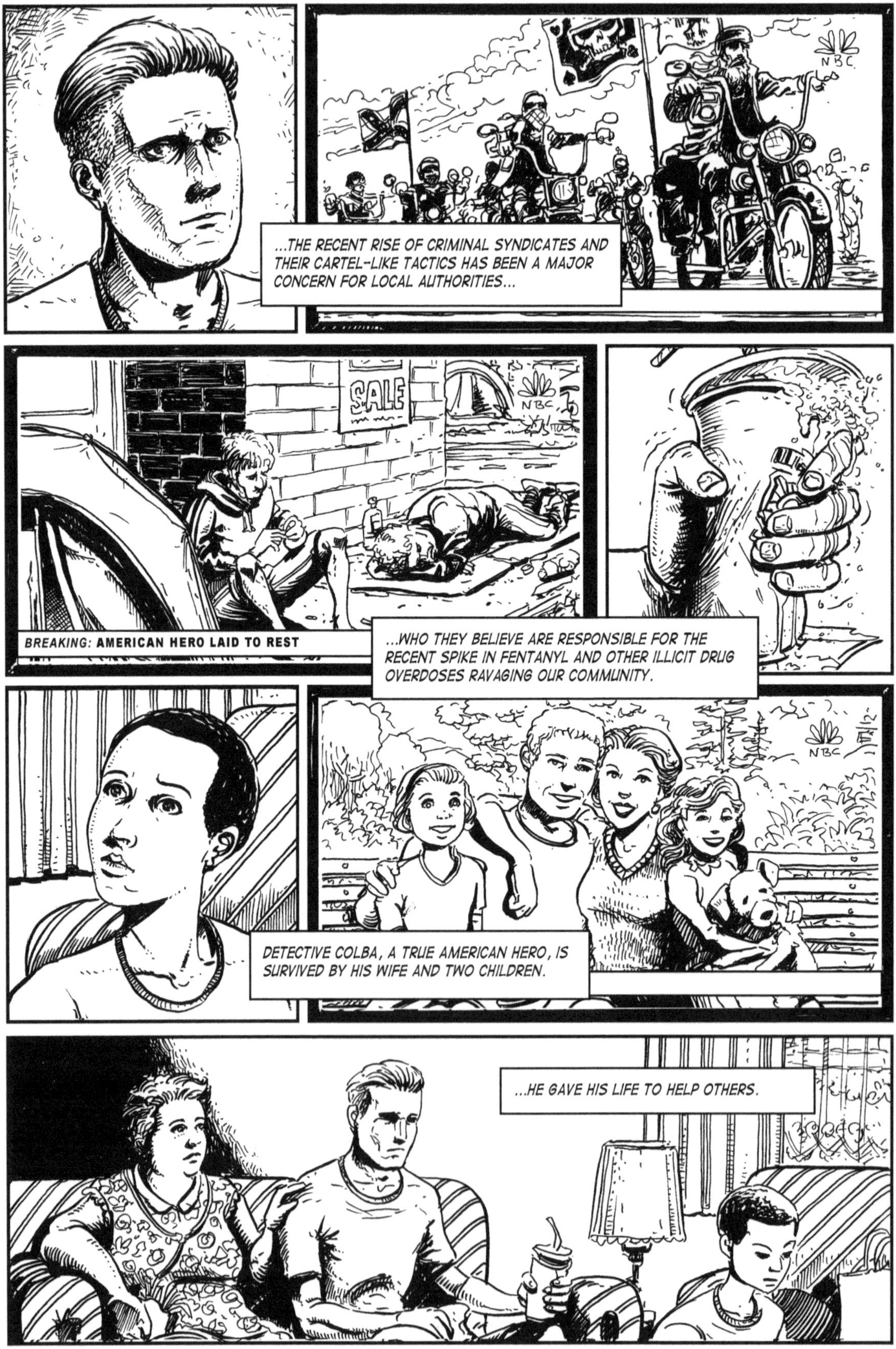

...THE RECENT RISE OF CRIMINAL SYNDICATES AND THEIR CARTEL-LIKE TACTICS HAS BEEN A MAJOR CONCERN FOR LOCAL AUTHORITIES...
BREAKING: AMERICAN HERO LAID TO REST
...WHO THEY BELIEVE ARE RESPONSIBLE FOR THE RECENT SPIKE IN FENTANYL AND OTHER ILLICIT DRUG OVERDOSES RAVAGING OUR COMMUNITY.
DETECTIVE COLBA, A TRUE AMERICAN HERO, IS SURVIVED BY HIS WIFE AND TWO CHILDREN.

...HE GAVE HIS LIFE TO HELP OTHERS.

A FUNERAL SERVICE WAS HELD THIS MORNING.
GENDER ISN'T REAL, IT'S A SOCIAL CONSTRUCT!
GENDER ISN'T REAL?
I TOLD HIM, YOU'RE A WHITE CISGENDER MALE, YOU HAVE NO RIGHT TO BE TALKING ABOUT ANY OF THESE ISSUES! IT'S TIME FOR HIM TO LISTEN.
IT'S A SOCIAL CONSTRUCT.

WHY DON'T YOU GO TEST YOUR THEORIES IN THE MIDDLE EAST?
OR MAYBE I CAN JUST WHIP OUT MY DICK AND I PROVE IT TO YOU?

RING RING
Unknown Caller
mobile

I TOLD YOU TO STOP CALLING ME!

I DON'T TRUST ANYTHING YOU HAVE TO SAY!

RING
RING
RING
RING
RING
RING
RING
RING
Decline
Acc
RING
RING
RING
RING
RING
RING

I DON'T CARE ABOUT COLBA!
THEY CALLED ME A KIKE. THEY FUCKING KNEW ABOUT ME!
I'M COMING FOR YOU NOW! YOU AND ALL YOUR NAZI FRIENDS!

HEY!!!

DID YOU JUST THREATEN TO RAPE MY FRIENDS?

BABE, YOUR FRIENDS ARE CRAZY.
THEY'RE JUST JEALOUS OF HOW PRETTY YOU ARE.

STATE TROOPER
OFFICER PALMER, WE HAVE A SPECIAL DELIVERY FOR YOU.
WELCOME BACK TO THE FORCE OLD FRIEND!

GOD...
I HOPE I DON'T
REGRET THIS.

SO THAT'S IT, HUH? YOU'VE DECIDED. YOU'RE GOING BACK TO BEING A COP.
YOU HAVEN'T THOUGHT ANY MORE ABOUT THE LAWSUIT?
IT'S THE ONLY WAY TO FIND OUT WHO KILLED YOUR MOTHER.
THAT'S NOT GOING TO BRING HER BACK, DAD. IT'S NOT GOING TO GIVE US THE TIME WE LOST.
MONEY ISN'T GOING TO BRING HER BACK EITHER, KAIA.

CHAPTER FOUR

Boxed Wine and BROKEN PROMISES

ALEXANDER?
ALEXANDER BYRON...

I THINK I LOVE YOU.
WHO KEEPS TEXTING YOU?
BABE, ARE YOU AWAKE?

YOU LYING
PIECE OF SHIT!

THIS IS NBC WITH BREAKING NEWS...
...AL PALMER WAS RELEASED FROM PRISON THIS WEEK AFTER A REVIEW OF EVIDENCE WITHHELD IN HIS INITIAL TRIAL, PROVED HIS INNOCENCE AND GROSS CORRUPTION BY THE PROSECUTION AND D.A.
STATE TROOPER
...IT BREAKS MY HEART WHAT THEY DID TO HIM, AFTER LOSING HIS WIFE... AND ALL FOR THE OPTICS."
435 VERNON UNIT 419. 10-16, DOMESTIC DISTURBANCE.
THIS IS OFFICER PALMER. I'M ON IT.
OFFICER PALMER? WELCOME BACK, SIR!

I'M ONLY TWENTY! AND HE BOUGHT ME WINE!
YOU HAVE TO ARREST HIM!
HEY BABE, DID YOU SEE MY WATCH?
COULD YOU PLEASE DESCRIBE THE WINE IN QUESTION? WAS IT BOXED? JUGGED?
BOXED!

BOXED WINE. CHEAP SON-OF-A-BITCH.

THIS ISN'T FUNNY YOU GUYS.

COULD YOU PLEASE DESCRIBE THE COLOR OF THE WINE?
PINK.

HEY MARY BETH, CAN WE PLEASE GET THE SKETCH ARTIST OVER HERE TO 435 VERNON. WE NEED A MOCK UP OF SOME BOXED ROSE.

...THIS ISN'T A JOKE!
ARREST HIM OR I'M CALLING MY DADDY. HE'S A LAWYER IN LITTLE ROCK!
OH, NO. NOT ONE OF DEM FANCY BIG CITY LAWYERS!
HA, HA, HA
HEE, HA, HA
OFFICER PALMER, HERE. WHAT SEEMS TO BE THE PROBLEM?
HE SAID HE LOVED ME!

NO, I DIDN'T.

YOU'RE SUCH. AN ASSHOLE!
HE ALSO BOUGHT ME GOLDSCHLAGER AND FIREBALL! I'M UNDERAGE.
MA'AM, THAT IS A SERIOUS ACCUSATION.
THAT IS A SERIOUS ACCUSATION!
A GROWN-ASS MAN DRINKING FIREBALL?!

I DON'T DRINK FIREBALL.
YES, HE DOES!
WE DRANK FIREBALL. REMEMBER?
YOU CRIED ABOUT THE NAZIS AND TOLD ME ABOUT YOUR GRANDMA.
YOU SAID THAT YOU LOVED ME... ...THAT THERE WAS A GOVERNMENT CONSPIRACY AGAINST YOU.
WILL YOU GUYS PLEASE JUST ARREST ME ALREADY AND GET ME THE FUCK OUT OF HERE?
I'LL KILL HIIM!

YOU HAVE THE RIGHT TO REMAIN SILENT...

HA, HA, HA
...EVERYTHING YOU SAY OR DO CAN AND WILL BE USED AGAINST YOU...

IF YOU CANNOT AFFORD AN ATTORNEY, ONE WILL BE PROVIDED FOR YOU.

WAIT! I'M SORRY! I DIDN'T MEAN IT!

I LOVE YOU, BABE! I'LL WAIT FOR YOU!

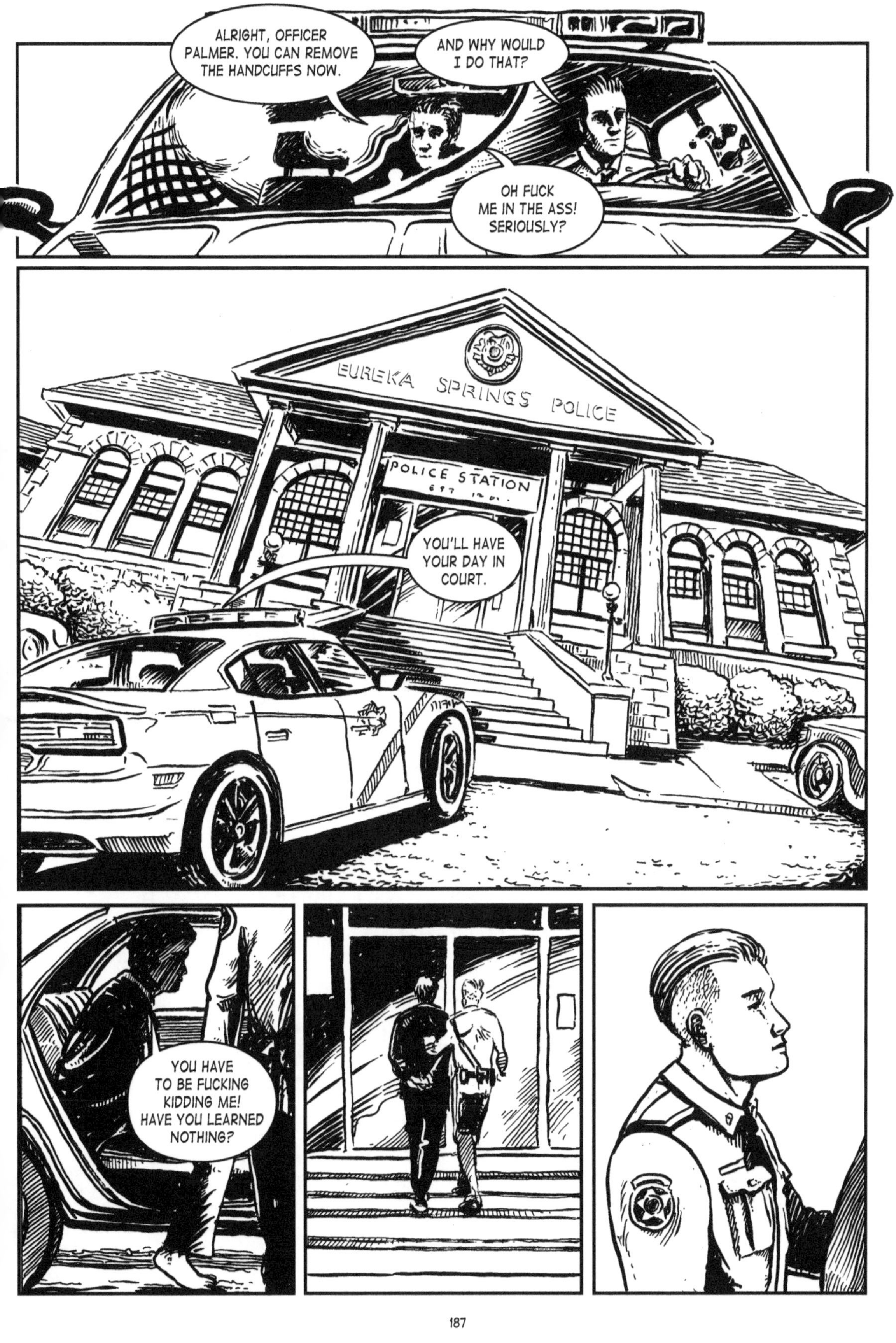

EUREKA SPRINGS POLICE
POLICE STATION
YOU'LL HAVE YOUR DAY IN COURT.

RECEPTION
CAN SOMEONE PLEASE TELL OFFICER DICKHEAD HERE, TO RELEASE ME?
HEE, HA, HA
HA, HA, HA

HOLDING CELLS
CL'K
189

GOOD TO SEE SOMEONE IS STILL DOING THEIR JOB AROUND HERE.
MARSHALL!
LOOK AT YOU, KID.
BACK ONLY ONE DAY, AND YOU ALREADY CAUGHT PUBLIC ENEMY NUMBER ONE.
190

THAT COCKY PRICK THINKS HE RUNS THIS PLACE JUST BECAUSE HE WAS IN AFGHANISTAN.
HEY MAN, DO YOURSELF A FAVOR, AND LET BYRON GO.
AND YOU ARE?
THIS IS DETECTIVE JONAH 'GRANOLA' ATKINS. FREER OF POLAR BEARS, COMMANDER OF THE SOCIAL JUSTICE WARRIORS.
THAT'S A BIT UNFAIR...
YES JONAH, EVERYTHING IS SO UNFAIR. PALMER CAN DEAL WITH OFFICER BYRON ANY WAY HE WANTS. BEEN A COP WAY LONGER THAN YOU.
NOW, COME ON.... LET'S GO FIND YOU A LUNA BAR. I THINK YOUR BLOOD SUGAR IS DROPPING.
BYRON IS... ALEXANDER BYRON?
YEAH! AND HE'S ONE OF THE FEW COPS HERE THAT ISN'T RACIST! HE'S THE ONE PERSON HERE THAT ACTUALLY RESPECTS MY PRONOUNS.
...BUT BYRON USED TO SELL DRUGS.

DRUGS THAT SHOULDN'T HAVE BEEN ILLEGAL IN THE FIRST PLACE...AN EXCUSE TO ARREST PEOPLE OF COLOR. AND WE'RE STOPPING THAT NOW.

PALMER, CAN I PLEASE HAVE A WORD?

LOOKS, LIKE THE CHIEF IS SAVING YOU FROM A LECTURE ON MARX AND 1619. LET'S CATCH UP LATER.

WELCOME BACK, KIDDO!

POLICE CHIEF
PALMER, HOW'S IT FEEL BEING BACK?
A BIT STRANGE I MUST ADMIT. I JUST MET AN OFFICER... ATKINS?
I'M SORRY. I KNOW IT'S ANNOYING. BUT PLEASE REFER TO HIM AS "THEY."
THEY? I THINK KAIA MIGHT HAVE SAID SOMETHING LIKE THAT.
I KNOW. I'M VERY SORRY. I KNEW SHE WAS STRUGGLING. I JUST DIDN'T REALIZE IT WAS "CHANGE HER PRONOUNS" BAD. WE'LL GET HER SOME HELP.
WHAT DOES IT ALL MEAN?
BESIDES IT BEING AN ALL OUT ASSAULT ON REALITY? IT'S BETTER TO JUST DO WHATEVER THEY SAY. THIS GENERATION IS FRAGILE. IF YOU CALL THEM THE WRONG PRONOUNS...SOMETIMES THEY KILL THEMSELVES.
ARE YOU SERIOUS?!
SOME ARE CATS NOW! FROGS EVEN. BUT THAT'S NOT WHAT I WANTED TO TALK TO YOU ABOUT...
...JIM PICKETT. I DON'T GIVE A SHIT ABOUT MY CAREER ANYMORE. I JUST WANT TO CATCH THIS SON OF A BITCH. THE DIRTY OFFICER IN QUESTION IS NAMED ALEXANDER BYRON.

THE MAN I JUST ARRESTED?

WHY DID YOU ARREST OFFICER BYRON?
HE GAVE LIQUOR TO A MINOR. THE GIRL WAS TWENTY.

THAT MAN IS NOTHING BUT TROUBLE! ANYWAY, HE'S THE ONE YOU WILL BE INVESTIGATING.

HE AND HIS PARTNER WERE UNDERCOVER WITH THE WHITE LIONS. HIS PARTNER WAS JUST KILLED BY THEM...
BUT I THINK IT WAS A DIRTY TRICK. I THINK THEY ARE BOTH DIRTY WORKING BEHIND MY BACK WITH ANOTHER DEPARTMENT.
I'M PUTTING YOU AND BYRON TOGETHER. I WANT YOU TO BE MY EYES AND EARS....
FIND A WAY TO EXPOSE HIM.

YES, SIR...

YOU THINK BYRON HAD SOMETHING TO DO WITH MY WIFE'S DEATH?
AT LEAST THE MEN HE'S IN BED WITH. BUT I SHOULD WARN YOU... BEING A COP ISN'T WHAT IT WAS BEFORE YOU WENT AWAY. THESE DAYS, YOU HAVE TO BE A SAINT OR HALF-RETARDED. MOST OF MY BEST MEN HAVE ALREADY QUIT. AND LIKE I SAID, THE OTHERS ARE HALF-RETARDED.
I'M SO SORRY TO DO THIS TO YOU...
...I FEEL LIKE I MANIPULATED YOU TO GET YOU BACK...
...BUT I CAN'T TRUST ANYONE ANYMORE. HALF MY BOYS THINK "THE SOUTH WILL RISE AGAIN."
...AND THE OTHER HALF WANT TO STERILIZE KIDS AND BRING FORTH THE COMMUNIST REVOLUTION.
IT'S GOTTEN SO BAD SINCE YOU LEFT... I NEED YOU, PALMER.

WHEN IT'S COLD IN THE WINTER I SLEEP IN THE JAILS, WHEN THERE'S WORK IN THE MOUNTAIN I'M OUT ON THE TRAIL,
JESUS CHRIST, BYRON!
CLICK KLUNK
OH, HEY THERE, CHIEF!
GET YOUR ASS UP!
YOU'RE LOOKING PARTICULARLY SLENDER TODAY. DID SOMEONE GROOM YOUR MOUSTACHE FOR YOU?

POLICE
CHIEF

FUCK THIS SHIT!
I'M NOT WORKING
WITH HIM!

YOU'RE TRYING
TO SABOTAGE MY
INVESTIGATION!

HE IS GOING WITH
YOU. END OF STORY!
OR I SHUT THE WHOLE
THING DOWN!

HE'S BEEN BACK
ONE DAY! SHOULDN'T
HE AT LEAST ISSUE
SOME PARKING
TICKETS FIRST?!

HE'S ALREADY MADE
ONE ARREST. AND I'VE
PROMOTED HIM TO SECOND
LIEUTENANT DETECTIVE
FIRST GRADE. THAT MAKES
HIM YOUR SUPERIOR.

YOU DON'T UNDERSTAND WHAT WE'RE DEALING WITH. IF HE GETS KILLED, IT'S ON YOU.

WE LEAVE TOMORROW.

LEAVE WHERE?
THE SAME PLACE YOU WANTED TO INVESTIGATE ALL THOSE YEARS AGO... HOT SPRINGS.

HELLO?
DAD! THIS IS SAM HARKENS.
MR. HARKENS. I'M SO HAPPY TO FINALLY MEET YOU!

MY FAMILY IS SO GRATEFUL FOR EVERYTHING YOU'VE DONE. I PRAY FOR YOU EVERYDAY.
YOU'RE VERY WELCOME.
ARE YOU STAYING FOR DINNER?!
I WISH I COULD. BUT I HAVE A PRIOR ENGAGEMENT.
SEVEN AND I WERE WAITING FOR YOU TO DISCUSS HOW BEST TO PROCEED WITH THE LAWSUIT...
LAWSUIT?
AGAINST THE DEPARTMENT.
I DON'T WANT TO SUE ANYONE.
OUR FAMILY DESERVES RETRIBUTION. THEY TOOK TEN YEARS FROM YOU. I DIDN'T HAVE A FATHER BECAUSE OF THEM. THEY RUINED OUR LIVES!

KAIA, I TOLD YOU. THERE ISN'T GOING TO BE A LAWSUIT.

JUST LISTEN TO HIM, DAD. IF IT WASN'T FOR SAM, YOU'D STILL BE IN JAIL. WHAT HAPPENED TO "FUCK THE GOVERNMENT?"

IF THIS IS ABOUT MONEY, I'M NOT INTERESTED.

OUR PERCENTAGE GOES TO HELPING OTHER PEOPLE LIKE YOU IN THE INNOCENCE PROJECT.

THANK YOU, BUT NO. I AM GOING BACK TO WORK. IT WOULD BE UNETHICAL TO SUE THEM NOW.
I HAVE A JOB TO DO.

DAD WILL YOU JUST...
I'M SORRY, KAIA. BUT SOMEONE YOUR AGE WOULND'T UNDERSTAND.

SOMEONE MY AGE?! AND, DON'T CALL ME KAIA. MY NAME IS SEVEN!
I HEARD ABOUT THAT. IS THAT LIKE... ...A GAY THING?

...BECAUSE I LOVE YOU NO MATTER WHAT. I JUST DON'T GET THE WHOLE "THEY"... THAT MEANS MULTIPLE PEOPLE.

I DON'T GIVE A FUCK WHAT YOU THINK BECAUSE YOU'RE A CIS-WHITE MALE! YOU HAVEN'T HAD TO SUFFER THEY SAME KIND OF ADVERSITY AS PEOPLE LIKE ME.

KAIA?!

MY NAME IS NOT KAIA! IT'S SEVEN! I'M NON-BINARY!

CAN YOU EXPLAIN?
IT'S NOT THAT DIFFICULT.

IT MEANS I DON'T CONFORM TO THE PRONOUNS A WHITE PATRIARCHAL SOCIETY HAS INFLICTED ON ME. I'M GENDER NON-CONFORMING. SO PLEASE DON'T CALL ME KAIA ANYMORE. MY NAME IS SEVEN.

BUT YOUR MOTHER AND I GAVE YOU THAT NAME.

MY MOTHER IS DEAD.

I'M SORRY. SEVEN. I'LL CALL YOU WHATEVER YOU WANT. BUT...

BANG

BANG
204

NORMA! NO!
AAAAAAAAH!!!
I'VE BEEN SHOT!
GET OUT OF THE WAY, Y'ALL! I'M SENDING THIS CROOKED LAWYER BACK TO HELL!
CLICK

NANA! WHAT HAVE YOU DONE?!
I'M JUST TRYING TO PROTECT YOU.
AM I GOING TO DIE?
YOU'LL BE FINE. IT WAS JUST BIRD SHOT.
CALL AN AMBULANCE!!!
Cancel
Emerger

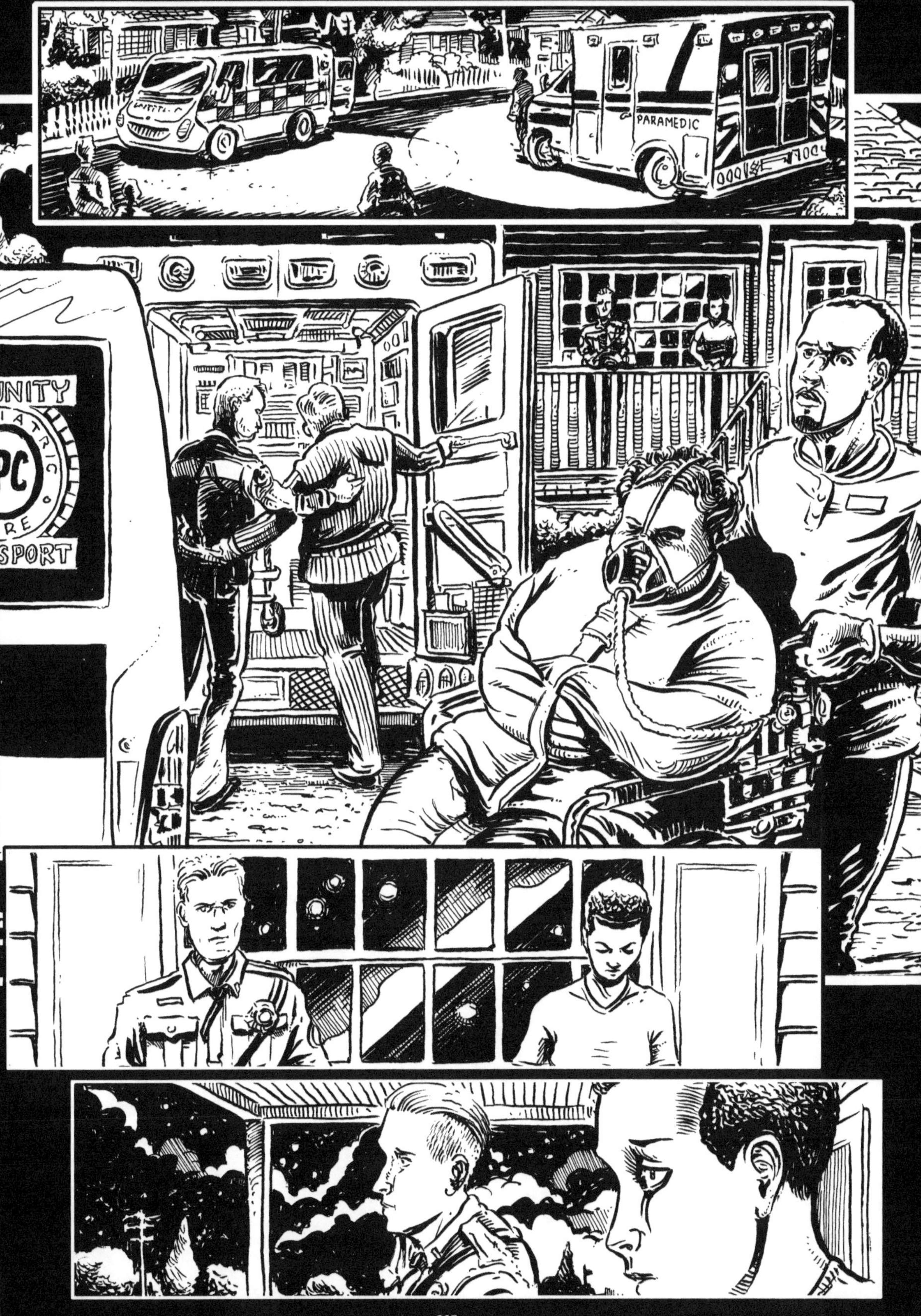
PARAMEDIC
UNITY
PC
SPORT

I'M SORRY, SEVEN, BUT THIS IS BIGGER THAN US.

THE BOAR IS STILL OUT THERE KILLING PEOPLE. IT WASN'T JUST YOUR MOTHER.

I'M SORRY I YELLED AT YOU. THAT I NEVER TOLD YOU ABOUT MY NEW IDENITY.

THAT'S OKAY. BUT RIGHT NOW I JUST WANT TO FIND OUT WHO KILLED YOUR MOTHER. I CAN'T DO THAT IF WE'RE INVOLVED IN A LAWSUIT WITH THE DEPARTMENT.

AND WHAT ABOUT NANA? HOW ARE WE GOING TO PAY TO TAKE CARE OF HER? THEY'LL MAKE HER LIVE IN A FACILITY NOW.

WE'LL FIGURE SOMETHING OUT. WE ALWAYS DO.

SHE ALWAYS THOUGHT YOU WERE INNOCENT, YOU KNOW?
NEVER REALLY BELIEVED WHAT I WAS TELLING HER...NOT UNTIL SHE STARTED TO LOSE HER MIND.
THIS DISEASE IS NOT HER. AND WE'LL ALWAYS TAKE CARE OF HER. I MADE A PROMISE TO HER.
I WILL NOT BE MADE A LIAR.

WHAT ARE THESE?

WHEN I WAS YOUNGER, I USED TO REPLY TO ALL YOUR LETTERS. A PART OF ME ALWAYS BELIEVED YOU WERE INNOCENT. BUT I NEVER SENT THEM. HERE .

I'LL READ EVERY SINGLE ONE.

JUST BE SAFE, DAD. I CAN'T LOSE YOU AGAIN.

LATER THAT NIGHT...
A.P. INTERVIEW
A-K
PALMER CASE
-forensic findings
-DNA sample...
-Ballistics
CONFIDENT...
AUTOPSY RESULTS S.P.
CORONERS FINDINGS
WITNESS Statement
WHITE LIONS
2009
£ 3/9
Palmer Case
Crime
Scene
Photos
and
analysis

210

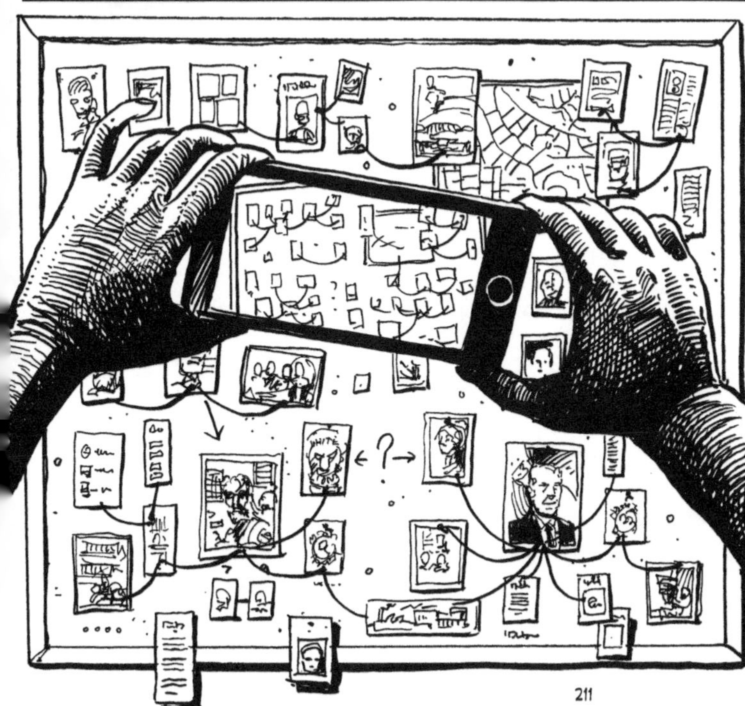

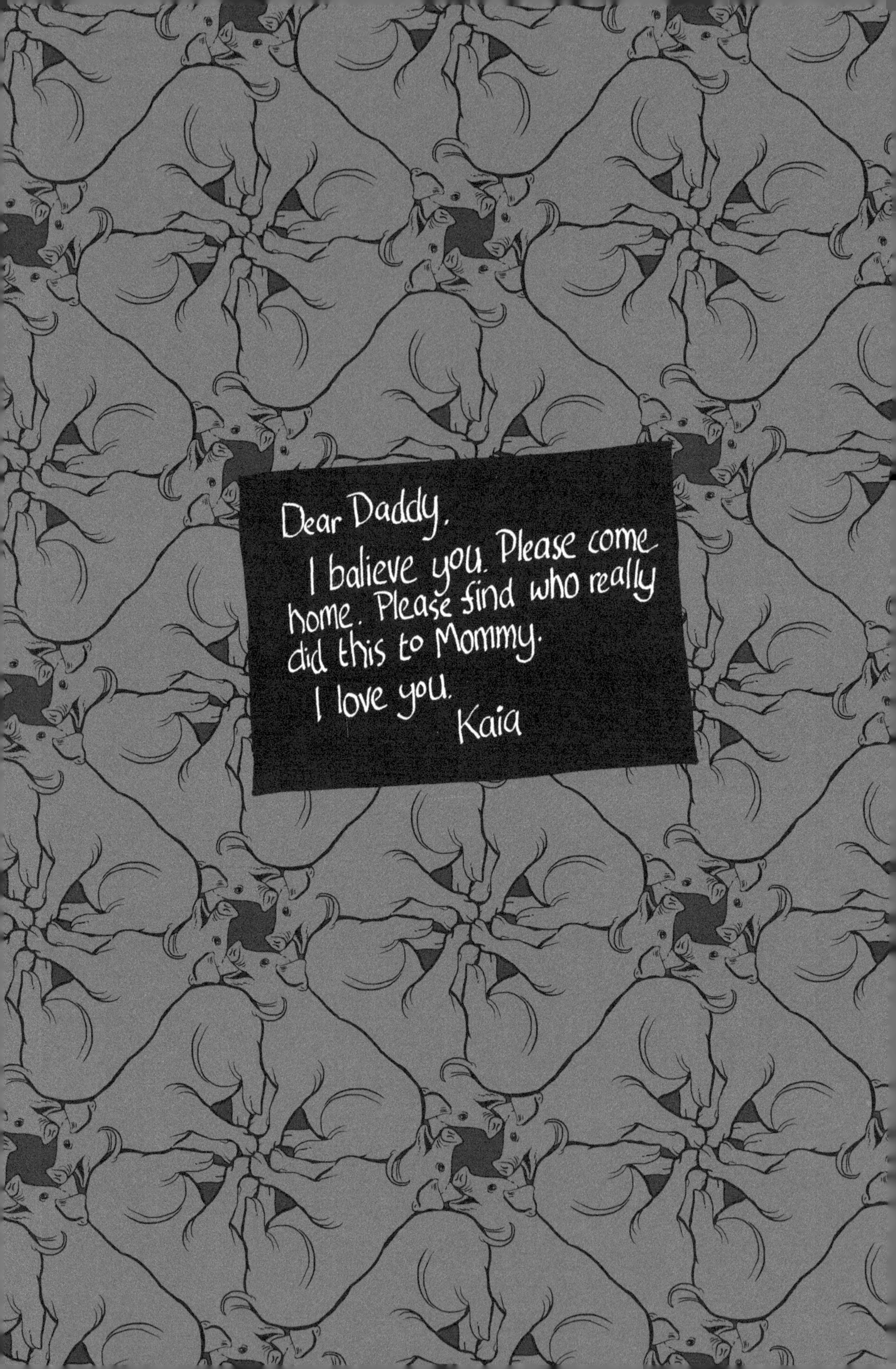
Dear Daddy,
I believe you. Please come home. Please find who really did this to Mommy.
I love you.
Kaia

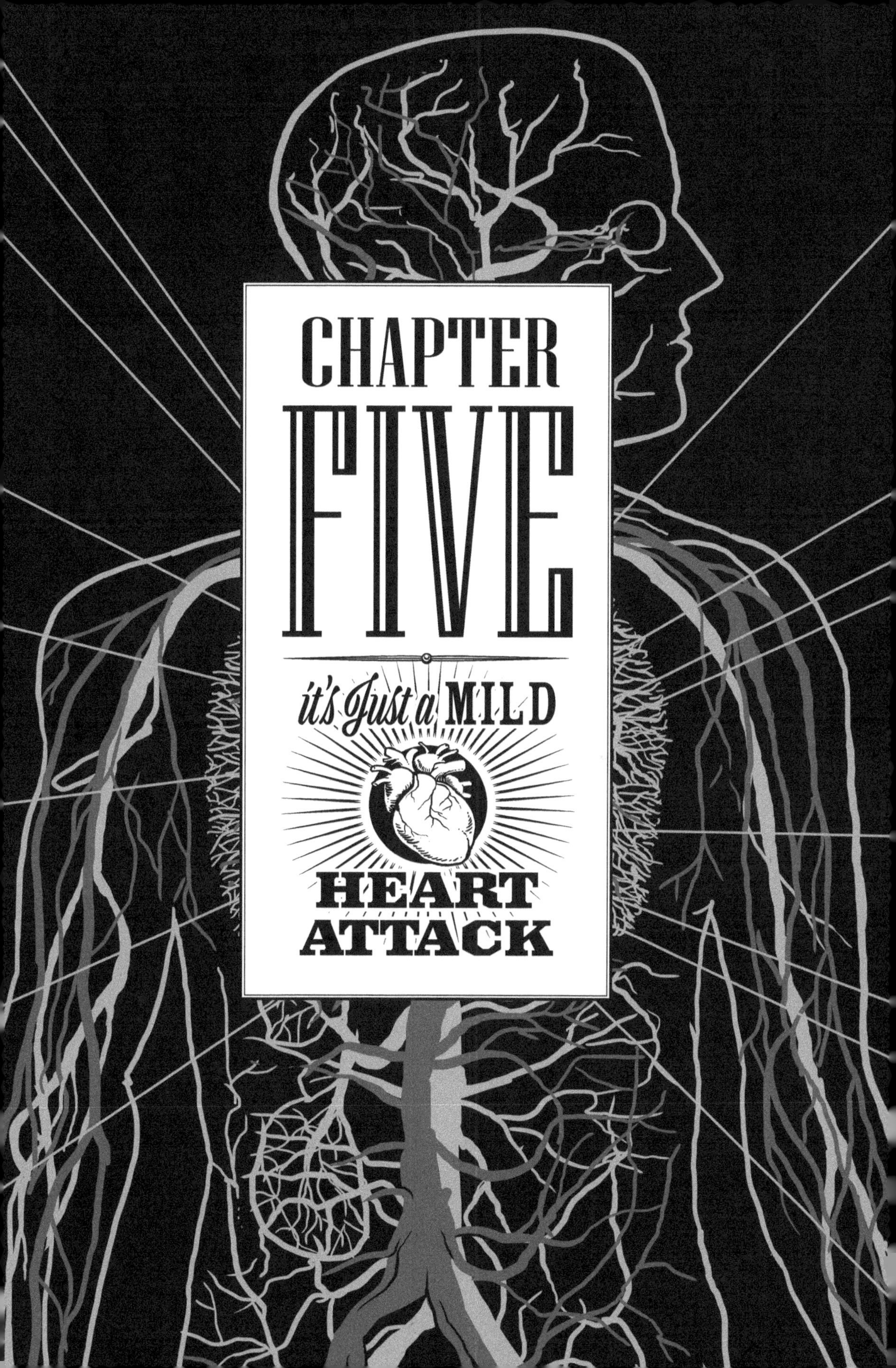

CHAPTER
FIVE
it's Just a MILD
HEART
ATTACK

THE NEXT MORNING...

WHO THE FUCK ARE YOU?
YOU MUST BE, KAIA.
MY NAME IS SEVEN.
SEVEN, THIS IS MY NEW PARTNER.
I REMEMBER THIS PRICK. YOU SHOULDN'T TRUST HIM!
YOU ALWAYS SAID NOT TO TRUST THE GOVERNMENT! WELL, HE'S THE GOVERNMENT!
37

SHE'S RIGHT. I DO WORK FOR THE GOVERNMENT. I HATE MYSELF FOR IT.
WHERE ARE YOU TAKING HIM?
HE'S DRIVING US TO HOT SPRINGS.
KAIA...I MEAN, SEVEN... I HAVE TO DO THIS.
I LOVE YOU.
I'LL BE BACK SOON.
I WANT TO SUPPORT YOU. BUT I CAN'T BELIEVE YOU ARE SO QUICK TO FORGIVE THE RACIST INSTITUTION THAT DID THIS TO YOU...
...WE NEED TO SUE THEM!

THE SYSTEM ISN'T PERFECT. IT MAKES MISTAKES. BUT IT'S THE BEST WE GOT. HAVE YOU SEEN THE REST OF THE WORLD?
IT RUINED OUR LIVES! THIS IS OUR CHANCE TO BE A FAMILY AGAIN. FOR YOU TO FINALLY BE MY FATHER. WITH THAT MONEY WE COULD FIGURE OUT WHAT HAPPENED TO MOM OURSELVES.
I'VE ALWAYS BEEN YOUR FATHER.
NO, YOU HAVEN'T! THEY TOOK YOU AWAY FROM ME AND BRAINWASHED ME TO HATE YOU.
THEY KILLED HER!
THAT'S WHY I HAVE TO DO THIS. TO CATCH THE MEN THAT ARE REALLY RESPONSIBLE.

PLEASE, DON'T GO, DAD! DON'T LEAVE ME AGAIN!
NOTHING IS EVER GOING TO TAKE ME AWAY AGAIN. I PROMISE.
I WANT TO BELIEVE THAT!
I'M DOING THIS FOR HER. FOR ALL OF US. I'LL BE BACK SOON.
BUT MOM IS GONE. AND NOTHING IS EVER GOING TO BRING HER BACK. IT'S JUST YOU AND ME NOW, DAD.

NOTHING IS GOING TO STOP US FROM BEING A FAMILY AGAIN. I PROMISE.

... DON'T WORRY. THIS GENDER SHIT WILL BLOW OVER. IT'S BEST TO JUST PLAY ALONG. HAVE FUN WITH IT...
...JONAH THINKS I LIKE HIM. *HA!* HE CAN IDENTIFY AS A KANGAROO FOR ALL I CARE.
I DON'T THINK HELPING SOMEONE LIE TO THEMSELVES IS HELPFUL...

WE ALL LIE TO OURSELVES IN SOME WAY. SO...YOU'RE REALLY NOT ANGRY ABOUT WHAT THEY DID TO YOU?

YOU'RE NOT ANGRY ABOUT WHAT THEY DID TO YOU?

"RESIST NOT EVIL."

YOU'RE A COP. YOU RESIST EVIL FOR A LIVING.

MATTHEW 5:39

THAT'S THE BEST YOU GOT? THAT'S SO BORING! I THOUGHT YOU'D AT LEAST HAVE SOMETHING INTERESTING TO SAY. YOU'RE SLEEPWALKING THROUGH LIFE, MAN. YOU WALK AROUND HERE LIKE SOME KIND OF MOROSE ZOMBIE.
IS THERE A PERSON INSIDE THERE AT ALL?

I KNOW THERE'S LIQUOR INSIDE THAT!

WHAT?!

IT'S ORANGE JUICE.

JESUS
loves you

DID YOU KNOW COCAINE HAS THE SAME EFFECT ON YOUR BRAIN AS FALLING IN LOVE?

PUT YOUR HEAD IN A BRAIN SCANNER...
LOVE? COCAINE?
...YOU WOULDN'T BE ABLE TO TELL THE DIFFERENCE.
PUT THAT AWAY OR I'M TAKING YOU BACK TO THE STATION!
I'M KIDDING! RELAX!
IT'S BAKING SODA! TASTE IT.

WHOAH!
THAT'S IT!

MEANWHILE...

Blood Alcohol Results
- too drunk to perform
sexually
QUANTITY
Evidence of 0.08% Alcohol
Detector Signal
Presence of Alcohol
Internal
Standard
Retention Time
1.18 min
1.5 Peak Rpt
0.5
exerpt from pathology report 1/28

No DNA Evidence
from Crime Scene
exerpt from CSI report
dated 5/28

TREVON ● DAVIS
Who was he? - Investor
- Wealthy
- Ladies Man
- Alcoholic

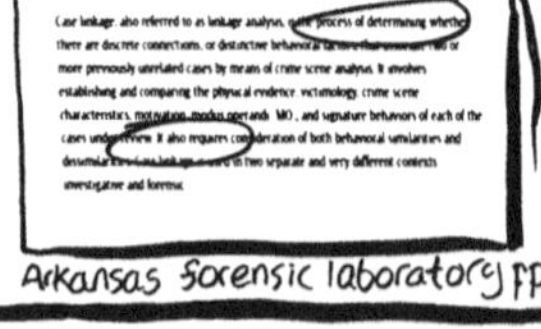

Evidence suggests body was mov
Arkansas forensic laboratory rpt.

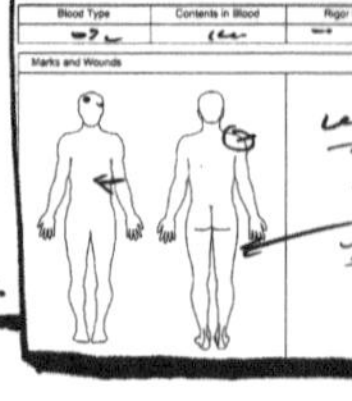

♡ Mum ♡
No DNA from Trevon on Mum
excerpt from CSI report dated 5/28
♡ miss you mum ♡♡♡
Where did they meet?
- work connections? X
- Social network connections X
- Mutual friendships? X
No Geographic connection
No Alcohol in Bloodstream
Pathology 20/2.
Not drinking due to pregnancy.
Rest in Peace
DNA shows Dad was father of baby.
Post mortem Exam. 20/3
AT the JK?
GOOGLE SEARCH: TREVON DAVIS
FACEBOOK SEARCH: TREVON DAVIS
FB FRIENDS SEARCH: KEISHA DAVIS
GOOGLE SEARCH: KEISHA DAVIS PUBLIC RECORDS
SEARCH: KEISHA DAVIS ADDRESS

IT HAS TO DO WITH DOPAMINE. THE BRAIN IS BASICALLY JUST A SUPER SMART DRUG MACHINE.

A MACHINE CANNOT TELL WHETHER YOU ARE IN LOVE OR NOT.

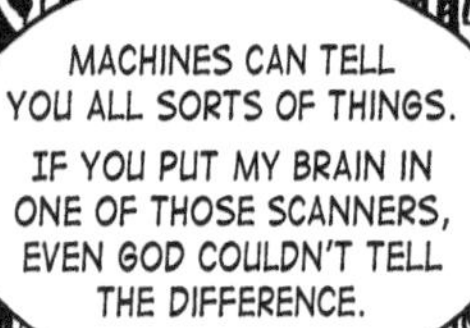

MACHINES CAN TELL YOU ALL SORTS OF THINGS.
IF YOU PUT MY BRAIN IN ONE OF THOSE SCANNERS, EVEN GOD COULDN'T TELL THE DIFFERENCE.
ONLY PEOPLE CAN KNOW IF THEY ARE IN LOVE. NOT MACHINES. BE CAREFUL IN BRINGING THE KINGDOM OF GOD TO EARTH. "NO ONE COMES TO THE FATHER EXCEPT THROUGH ME"

AND ALSO MACHINES AND COCAINE.

YOU'VE OBVIOUSLY NEVER BEEN IN LOVE.

I'VE BEEN IN LOVE....ONCE.

WHAT HAPPENED TO HER?

CHEVROLET

SHE TURNED OUT TO BE A LYING BITCH....

WHEN I GOT BACK FROM MY SECOND TOUR...SHE WAS GONE. I EVEN HACKED THE POLICE DATA BASE TRYING TO FIND HER.
YOU WHAT?!
SHE ALWAYS USED TO TALK ABOUT THESE SWIMMING PIGS IN THE BAHAMAS. IMAGINE THAT. SWIMMING PIGS! YOU CAN'T MAKE THAT SHIT UP.
I THOUGHT THAT'S WHERE SHE MIGHT BE. BUT I LATER FOUND OUT SHE JUST MARRIED THIS RICH GUY FOR HIS MONEY.
DON'T JUDGE HER!
THERE'S THIS CRAZY NOTION OUT THERE THAT IT'S SOMEHOW EASY TO MAKE MONEY! IT'S NOT. WE BOTH DID THE BEST WE COULD WITH WHAT WE HAD.
AMERICA IS THE RICHEST EMPIRE THAT HAS EVER EXISTED AND YET THE POOR ARE STILL LURED INTO THIS IMMIGRANT FANTASY.
THIS IDEOLOGY THAT WE ARE ALL GOING TO MAKE IT. BUT WE'RE NOT. THE POOR ARE FETISHIZED. AND THE MIDDLE CLASS GETS FUCKED THE WORST!

DID YOU LOVE YOUR WIFE?
OF COURSE I DID.

EVEN THOUGH SHE WAS CHEATING ON YOU?
WATCH YOUR MOUTH!

SERIOUSLY? BETWEEN YOU AND ME.... THAT DIDN'T CHANGE ANYTHING? AND THEN YOU EVEN GOT BLAMED FOR IT.
I TRUST IN THE FATHER. FAITH WILL BE SERVED. HERE OR IN THE NEXT.

I DON'T KNOW. MAYBE YOU REALLY DID KILL HER.

I DID NOT KILL MY WIFE!
SHE MIGHT NOT HAVE BEEN PERFECT BUT I LOVED HER.
I STILL LOVE HER.
I'M KIDDING. I'VE SEEN THE EVIDENCE. YOU'RE JUST AN IDIOT FOR LETTING THEM GET AWAY WITH IT.
STOP THAT!
I DID NOT KILL MY WIFE!

AAAAAAH
CHOOOO!!!

Ha Ha
Ha
Cough
sniff

HaHa

HeHe
He
twitch
twitch

Welcome
to
HOT SPRINGS

MY HEART!
I THINK I'M HAVING A HEART ATTACK.

HELLO?
HI, YOU DON'T KNOW ME BUT—
I KNOW WHO YOU ARE. PLEASE COME IN.
I AGREE. AS A CRT LAW PROFESSOR...
IT'S CRAZY THEY REOPENED HIS CASE!
RIGHT. YOU SAID THE POLICE ALREADY STOPPED BY. WHAT DID THEY ASK YOU?

THEY MOSTLY WANTED TO KNOW ABOUT THIS STRIP CLUB HE USED TO GO TO. LIKE THAT'S A CRIME!

WHY WOULD THEY BE INTERESTED IN A STRIP CLUB?

WE'RE FROM ATLANTA IT'S JUST PART OF THE CULTURE THERE. THEY'RE JUST TRYING TO MAKE HIM LOOK BAD.
WHICH STRIP CLUB?
THE 'PINK GOAT'.
CAN YOU TELL ME MORE ABOUT TREVON? WHAT WAS HE LIKE?
HANDSOME, FUNNY, VERY CHARMING. IT'S PROBABLY WHY YOUR MOTHER LIKED HIM.
THAT'S THE THING I WANTED TO TALK TO YOU ABOUT...
I DON'T THINK THEY KNEW EACH OTHER.
WAIT...YOU'RE ON THEIR SIDE?...
...YOU THINK YOUR FATHER IS INNOCENT?
YOU'RE A LAWYER. JUST LOOK AT WHAT I BROUGHT YOU.

IT DOESN'T MATTER. I THOUGHT YOU AND I WERE ON THE SAME SIDE.

WE ARE! YOU WANT TO FIND OUT WHO KILLED YOUR BROTHER, I WANT TO FIND WHO KILLED MY MOM!

OUT!

SLAM

PINK GOAT

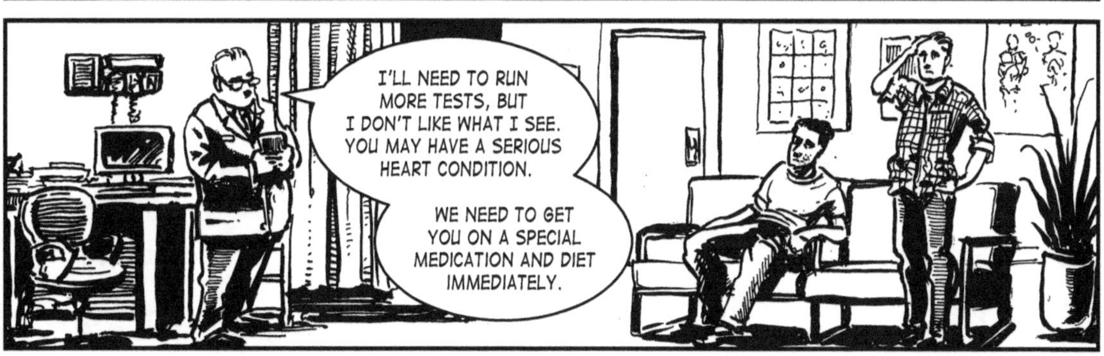

I DON'T THINK IT WAS A HEART ATTACK. YOU MOST LIKELY HAD A PANIC ATTACK.
BUT I FELT LIKE I WAS DYING!
MELANOMA

I'LL NEED TO RUN MORE TESTS, BUT I DON'T LIKE WHAT I SEE. YOU MAY HAVE A SERIOUS HEART CONDITION.
WE NEED TO GET YOU ON A SPECIAL MEDICATION AND DIET IMMEDIATELY.

SO BASICALLY IT WAS A GOOD THING HE HAD A PANIC ATTACK. NOW, WE KNOW HE HAS A HEART CONDITION.
FUNG
CHECK FOR
SIGNS

LATER THAT DAY...
SO WHAT'S THE PLAN?
TRANQUILLO.
WHAT ARE WE DOING HERE?
WE'RE GOING TO GET IN THE HOT TUB AND HAVE A FEW BEERS.
I'LL BE INSIDE.

HEY! COME ON, PALMER! HAVE A BEER.
SPLASH
YOU'VE NOT SHARED A SINGLE DETAIL WITH ME.
LET'S QUICKLY JERK EACH OTHER OFF AND THEN I'LL TELL YOU WHAT YOU WANT TO KNOW.
THIS ISN'T A JOKE TO ME.
I'M YOUR PARTNER. YOU AND I WE'RE ON THE SAME SIDE.
MY PARTNER IS DEAD. YOU'RE MY BABY SITTER. SO, IF I NEED MY ASS WIPED, I'LL LET YOU KNOW.

MOTIVE? Why kill Sarah?
- Was I the target?
- were they expecting to find me?
- Was the murder an accident?
- Was framing me a shitty attempt at covering up their mistake?
- What does Kaia remember? Did she hear anything?

crime
Gangs loc.

What does Kaia remember?   Did she hear anything?

DAD? IS EVERYTHING OKAY?
EVERYTHING IS FINE. I JUST WANTED TO LET YOU KNOW WE ARRIVED. HOW ARE YOU DOING?

GONNA TRY AND VISIT NANA TOMORROW.

TELL HER, WE'LL GET HER OUT OF THERE AS SOON AS WE CAN..

HEY, I'M SORRY TO ASK YOU THIS. BUT...WHAT DO YOU REMEMBER ABOUT THAT NIGHT?
...WHEN YOUR MOTHER...
I DON'T KNOW DAD...

... I THOUGHT I HEARD FIREWORKS. MAYBE THERE WAS YELLING. I DON'T KNOW...
I WAS SO SCARED...IT ALL FEELS LIKE A DREAM NOW.

THAT'S OKAY, THANKS SEVEN.
BE SAFE OUT THERE.

I WILL. I LOVE YOU.
I LOVE YOU, TOO.
PINK GOAT
243

THE GUY'S AN IDIOT! TRUST ME, YOU DO NOT WANT HIM OUT HERE. HE'S GOT THAT FOLKSY FORREST GUMP THING GOING ON. BUT HE MIGHT BE RETARDED.

WHO ARE THESE PEOPLE?

HEY GUYS! THIS IS MY VERY COOL BABY SITTER WHO LETS ME STAY UP SUPER LATE AND DRINK BEER NAKED IN THE HOT TUB WITH MY FRIENDS...

WELL DON'T JUST STAND THERE WITH YOUR HAND ON YOUR DICK, CLIMB ON IN AND SAY HELLO.

IS THAT POT?! BYRON, ARE YOU DOING DRUGS?!

OXY IS A DRUG. COCAINE IS A DRUG. ALCOHOL IS A DRUG. POT?!

MY GRANDMA SMOKES POT.
ACTUALLY, MARIJUANA IS A SCHEDULE ONE NARCOTIC...
WELL, MAYBE YOU TWO CAN TEAM UP, LAUNCH AN INVESTIGATION, AND ARREST MY GRANDMA.
MAYBE WE SHOULD.
PEDANTIC. THAT'S THE WORD YOU'RE LOOKING FOR.
YES! PEDANTIC. YOU'RE SO SMART.
YOU GUYS, LEAVE HIM ALONE. HE SEEMS LIKE HE MEANS WELL.
I KNEW YOU GUYS WOULD HIT IT OFF. OFFICER GARCIA HERE HAS A REAL STICK UP HER ASS TOO.
SPLASH
YOU GUYS ARE COPS?!
HOT SPRINGS PD. I THINK HE'S CUTE!

OKAY. BUT JUST BE CAREFUL. HE DID JUST GET OUT OF FEDERAL-POUND-ME-IN-THE-ASS PRISON FOR MURDERING HIS WIFE.
I DIDN'T KILL MY WIFE!
WHAT'S THE PLAN FOR TOMORROW?
TRANQUILLO. GET YOUR SUIT AND JUMP IN. AND WE'LL EXPLAIN IT TO YOU.
I DON'T HAVE A SUIT.
NO PROBLEMO!
LET ME BE YOUR CONDUCTOR AND YOU BE MY CABOOSE... ...CHOO, CHOO!
Ha Ha Ha Ha Ha Ha Ha Ha Ha Ha Ha Ha

MEANWHILE...
YOU RECOGNIZE THIS MAN?
HE WAS A REGULAR 10 YEARS AGO.
THE ONLY PERSON THAT ANCIENT HERE IS CRYSTAL.
CRYSTAL?
YES?
DO YOU KNOW THIS MAN?
IS THAT, TREVON? WOW! IT'S BEEN SO LONG!

HOW OFTEN WOULD HE COME IN?
I'M WORKING, DARLIN'.
I CAN PAY FOR A PRIVATE DANCE.
HE WAS OBSESSED WITH THIS ONE GIRL. ANGEL....
TWO OF THE GUYS THAT USED TO HANG WITH ANGEL, HELPED HIM OUT ONE NIGHT WHEN HE WAS BLACKOUT DRUNK... DROVE HIM HOME I GUESS. NEVER SAW HIM AGAIN.
YOU KNOW WHERE I CAN FIND HER?
A GIRL LIKE YOU SHOULD STAY AWAY FROM ANGEL.
WHAT DOES THAT MEAN?
THE TRAILER PARK, PAST THE WAFFLE HOUSE...
SHE GOT FIRED FROM HERE FOR HER "WHITE LIONS" SHIT.
THE WHITE LIONS?
THAT BITCH SCARED ME...
...SHE SCARED ALL OF US.
249

ANYTHING ELSE YOU CAN TELL ME?
TREVON WAS A NICE GUY. ME AND THE OTHER GIRLS REALLY LIKED HIM. HE ALWAYS TREATED US WITH RESPECT.
YOU KNOW WHICH TRAILER WAS ANGEL'S?
I'M SERIOUS! A YOUNG GIRL LIKE YOU SHOULD NOT GO OUT THERE...
THESE FOLKS AIN'T "TWITTER RACIST." THEY'RE THE REAL DEAL.
I UNDERSTAND. THANK YOU!

HOW IS BYRON CONNECTED TO JIM PICKET?
WHITE LIONS
Hot Springs
251

Why would they want to kill me?
- How close did they come?
- What scared them?
- Why so desperate?
LOCAL PIG FARM
MAJOR EXPANSION
I was investigating Jim Picket at the time
Imports par
from Mexic
connection
to cartels
Heavenly
Farms
Drugs must be tied to pig farms and maybe
Christian themeparks
252

AVACADO
Partnering with cartels? Human trafficking?
Recent investments in avacados
JIM PICKET NEW GOVERNOR
STRIP CLUBS
Pussy Cats
PINK GOAT
Chantelles
GIRLS GIRLS GIRLS
CREATION LAND
Picket's main fortune has come from 'Creation Land' theme parks throughout the south.
Initial money comes from inheritance Father owned various strip clubs

253

ZZZZ...
254

GET ONE
FREE!
Large
COLA!
CHEAP BRE
IMPLA
$$$$$
CELE
SCANDA
BABY
BUMP!

NO! NO!
AL, THEY AREN'T
UNDERSTANDING ME.
WHAT IS THIS?!

OUT of CONT
GRISH

RUN, CHILDREN!
RUN!!!

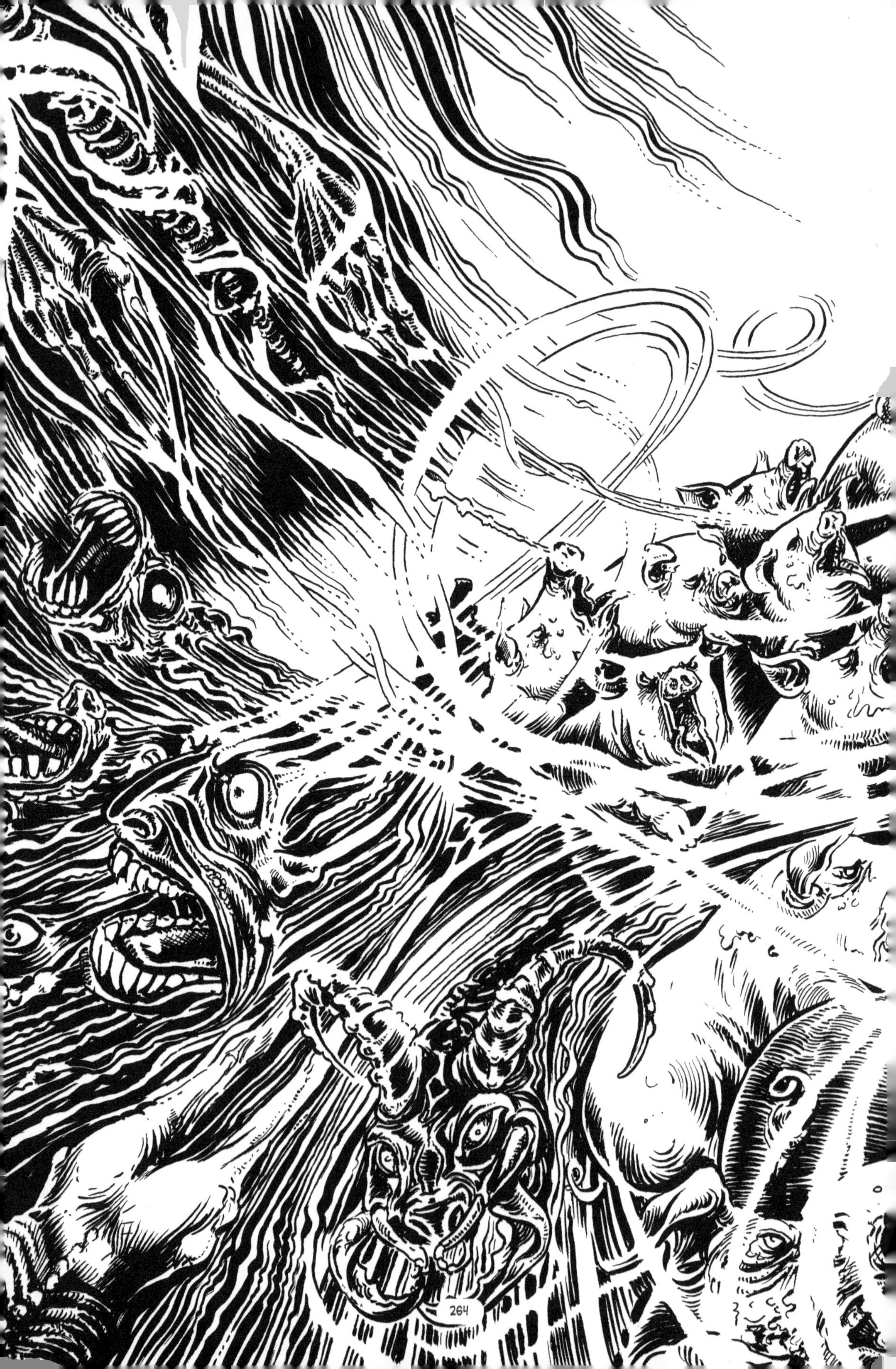

264

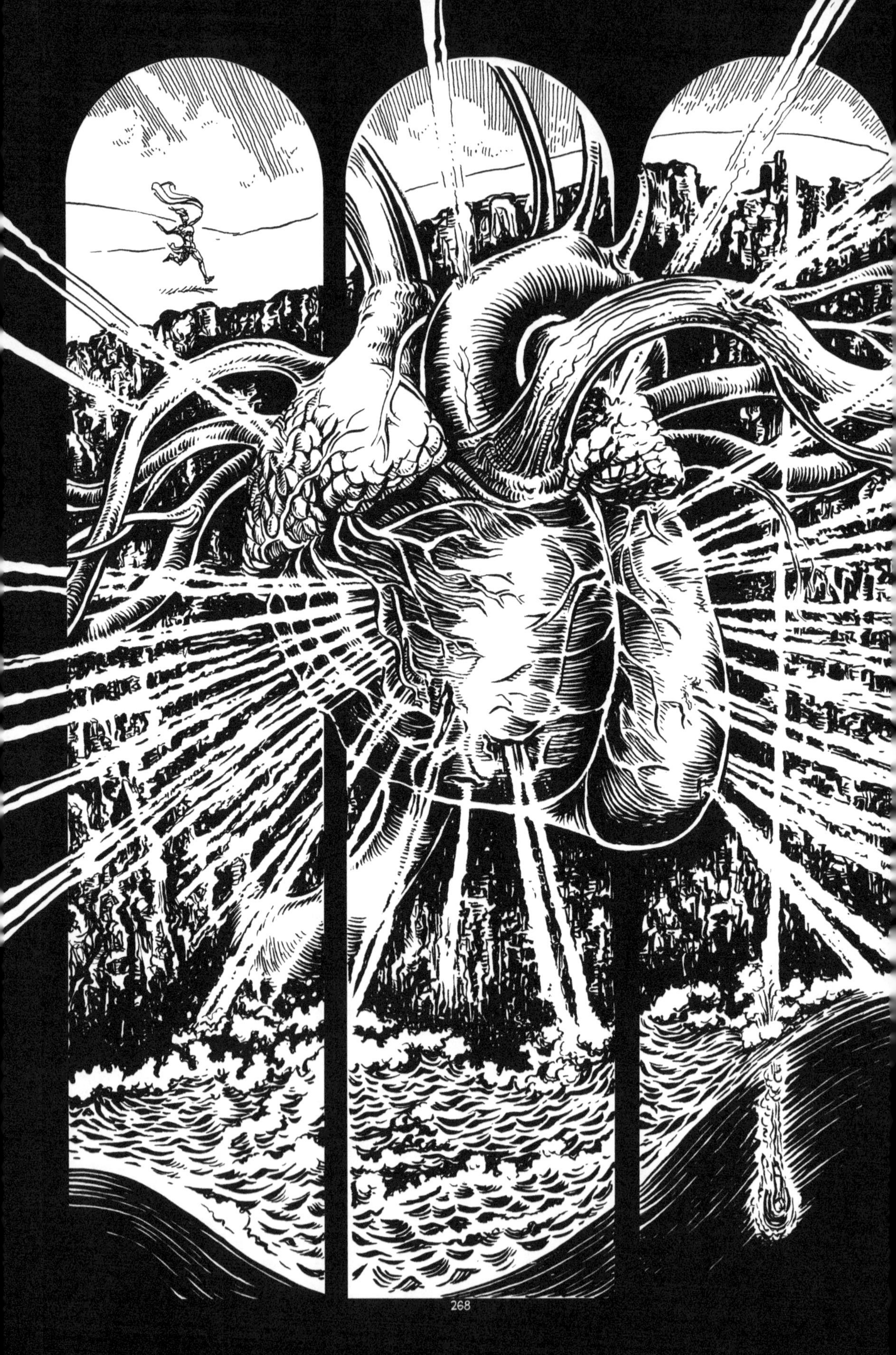

THE NEXT MORNING...

GASP

270

... I DON'T KNOW. STALL HIM. I'M ON MY WAY NOW TO THE STATION.

OH, HEY! GOOD MORNING. SLEEP WELL?

WHERE'S BYRON?
HE WENT WITH SAMANTHA TO MEET HER C.I... HE SAID TO LET YOU SLEEP.
UNBELIEVABLE!

271

COME ON.
I'LL DROP YOU OFF
ON MY WAY TO
THE STATION.

WHAT'S
GOING ON
HERE?

WE GOT A BIG
FEW DAYS AHEAD OF US.
THE DEA AND FBI ARE
ALREADY HERE, LOCKED
AND LOADED.

GOOD MORNING
BEAUTIFUL.

THE DEA AND THE FBI?

PRIDE
HE'S SUPPOSED
TO BE ALONE.

DON'T TAKE IT PERSONAL WITH BYRON. WE'RE ALL A BIT NERVOUS ABOUT SHARING INFORMATION WITH EUREKA SPRINGS P.D.
Y'ALL AS LEAKY AS A RUSTY BUCKET?
YOU TRUST BYRON?
I KNOW HE'S AT LEAST NOT A NAZI... CHIEF WHITE ON THE OTHER HAND?
CHIEF WHITE IS NOT A NAZI! YOU'RE TELLING ME HE'S ONE OF YOUR SUSPECTS?
IF WE'RE CROSSING SWORDS... YEAH, HE'S A PREETY BIG ONE...
THAT'S RIDICULOUS! CHIEF WHITE HAS A LONG HISTORY BEING A PROGRESSIVE POLICE CHIEF...
NOW, I DESERVE TO BE BROUGHT IN ON THIS. I WENT TO PRISON FOR THIS INVESTIGATION!
WHICH IS WHY I'M TAKING YOU TO BYRON. BUT YOU HAVE TO UNDERSTAND... WE HAVE A MOLE SOMEWHERE.
BYRON USED TO SELL DRUGS, YOU KNOW THAT? I ALMOST ARRESTED HIM.
ALMOST ONLY COUNTS IN HORSE SHOES AND HAND GRENADES. YOU EVER THINK BYRON MIGHT HAVE BEEN WORKING UNDERCOVER FOR THE DEA? NOW, WE'VE BEEN TRYING TO BUILD A CASE AGAINST JIM PICKET FOR YEARS BUT IT KEEPS GETTING SQUASHED...WE'RE SO CLOSE. IT'S VERY DELICATE...HE'S THE FUCKING GOVERNOR NOW! THE MORONS LOVE HIM.

CHAPTER SIX

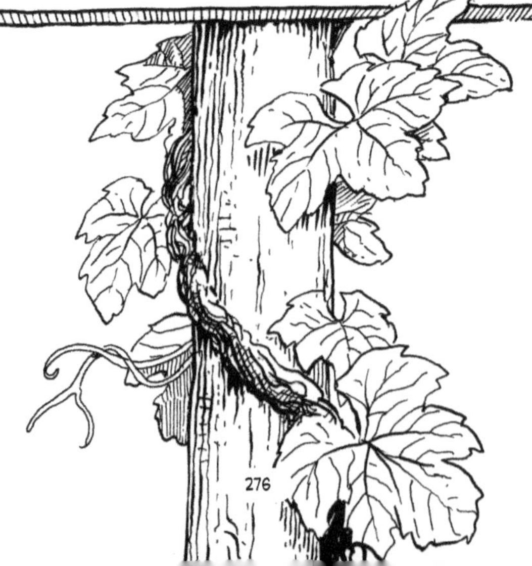

HI, I'M GOVERNOR JIM PICKET!
FUCK THE DEMOCRATS! THEY ARE TRYING TO REWRITE HISTORY.
DEMOCRATS SUPPORTED SLAVERY, STARTED THE KU KLUX KLAN, ENFORCED JIM CROW AND VOTED AGAINST THE CIVIL RIGHTS ACT OF THE 1960S AT HIGHER RATES THAN REPUBLICANS.
THE DEMOCRATS HAVE ALWAYS BEEN THE RACIST PARTY. DON'T BUY THEIR PROPAGANDA.
PEACHES
AND NOW, THEY WANT TO TAKE YOUR GUNS! YOUR FREEDOMS! YOUR GAS STOVES. YOUR RIGHT TO WORK THE LAND!
WELL, I'M A FARMER! I WORK THIS LAND WITH MY OWN TWO HANDS, LIKE MY DADDY DID BEFORE ME AND HIS DADDY DID BEFORE HIM.
MY OPPONENT, ON THE OTHER HAND, IS A CROOKED LAWYER WITH TIES TO BIG PHARMA AND GLOBALIST ELITES.
...AND CUT!

WHAT WAS WRONG WITH THAT ONE?

YOU CAN'T SAY "FUCK THE DEMOCRATS."
OH, I WAS JUST HAVING FUN.

AND MAYBE DON'T TALK SO MUCH ABOUT RACISM.
WE HAVE TO DO DAMAGE CONTROL.

IT'S BEST TO JUST IGNORE IT. DENY, DENY, DENY.
WE GOT TO DO SOMETHING ABOUT MY WIFE'S HISTORY TO MAKE THE VOTERS UNDERSTAND.

PLUS, THE BLACKS ARE FINALLY STARTING TO WAKE UP TO JUST HOW FUCKED THEY'VE BEEN BY THE DEMOCRATS.
THEY AREN'T AS DUMB AS YOU THINK. WE COULD GET THEIR VOTE!

279

280

TRYING TO LAY LOW. I'M SORRY, BABE. ALL THE HEADACHES I'VE CAUSED YOUR CAMPAIGN.
IT'S NOT YOUR FAULT. IT WAS JUST HOW YOU WERE RAISED. WE'LL MAKE PEOPLE SEE HOW YOU'VE CHANGED. YOU CAN BE AN INSPIRATION ON HOW OTHERS CAN PUT THAT KIND OF HATE BEHIND THEM.
I'M STILL SO ASHAMED. IT'S SO HORRIBLE.
AND THAT IS WHY THEY WILL FORGIVE YOU.

ARE WE STILL GOING TO HAVE NAUGHTY NIGHT TOMORROW?
BEEN LOOKING FORWARD TO NAUGHTY NIGHT ALL WEEK!
I'M MEETING THE GIRLS. I'LL BE BACK LATER.
282

S
WAFFLE HOUSE
WAFFLE HOUSE

EXCUSE ME?
YOU KNOW SOMEONE AROUND HERE, GOES BY ANGEL?
SHE DON'T LIVE HERE NO MORE. BUT THAT WAS HER PLACE BEHIND US.
THANK YOU.

I SAID NO MORE JOURNALISTS!
DON'T SHOOT!
WHAT DO YOU WANT?
I'M LOOKING FOR A WOMAN WHO USED TO LIVE HERE.
ANGEL? DO YOU KNOW HER?
I HAVEN'T HEARD ANYONE CALL HER THAT IN YEARS.
WAIT...WHY DID YOU THINK I WAS A REPORTER?
MY DAUGHTER. THEY FOUND OUT SHE WAS A NAZI...
...AND FOR THE RECORD, IT AIN'T MY FAULT. I NEVER HAD NO PROBLEM WITH COLORED PEOPLE.

WE PREFER PEOPLE OF COLOR.
LOOK, THERE AIN'T NO MORE DIRT TO DIG UP ON LO. IT'S ALL OUT THERE NOW.

WHO IS LO?
AND WHY DO PEOPLE CARE?

LORETTA PICKET. MARRIED TO JIM PICKET..
...THE GOVERNOR. RUNNING FOR RE-ELECTION.

I'M SORRY! WHAT?!

MY DAUGHTER AND THAT PIECE OF SHIT HUSBAND OF HERS HAVE ALL THE MONEY IN THE WORLD. BUT I AIN'T SEEN NONE OF IT! OH, SURE SHE'LL TELL YOU SHE GOT ME THIS TRAILER. BUT THE ONLY REASON I LOST IT IN THE FIRST PLACE WAS BECAUSE OF HER!

YOU STILL TALK TO HER?
I DON'T TALK TO THAT BITCH.

I'M LOOKING FOR TWO MEN SHE MIGHT HAVE KNOWN. CONNECTED TO HER FROM HER TIME AT THE PINK GOAT. RING ANY BELLS?
SHE USED TO RUN WITH A LOT OF MEN. GOOD AT CONTROLLING THEM, IF YOU KNOW WHAT I MEAN.
THESE TWO MEN MIGHT HAVE KILLED MY MOTHER.
WAIT! I KNOW YOU! YOU'RE THE DAUGHTER OF THE COP THAT KILLED HIS WIFE!
MY DAD DIDN'T DO IT. I'M TRYING TO FIND OUT WHO DID.
AND YOU THINK MY LO HAD SOMETHING TO DO WITH IT?
MAYBE...I DON'T KNOW. PROBABLY.

I WANT YOU TO LEAVE.
PLEASE, I'M SORRY! I JUST—
MY DAUGHTER MIGHT BE A NAZI, BUT SHE AIN'T NO MURDERER.
I SAID OUT!
23a

EDEN VALLEY
Wine Tasting
Session B.
:30am – 12:00 pm.
GOLD MEDAL
CHARDONNAY

THAT ISN'T SELF-SERVE!
GLUG GLUG
DON'T WORRY. I'M A COP.
WHAT ARE YOU, JAMES BOND? WE'RE SUPPOSED TO BE UNDERCOVER.
WHY ARE YOU ACTING SO NERVOUS?
I'M NOT NERVOUS.
HEY!! YOU FUCKING DITCHED ME!

WHOA! TAKE IT EASY WITH THE FIVE DOLLAR WORDS. THERE'S A LADY PRESENT.
BOTH OF YOU, COOL IT.

I'M YOUR PARTNER.
SAMANTHA IS MY PARTNER. YOU'RE AN IDIOT.

WHY ARE YOU HIDING THIS CI?

IT'S SAMANTHA'S CI. I'M JUST HERE TO HELP...
...NOW THIS GORGEOUS CHARDONNAY IS FINALLY OPENING UP.

IF YOU WANT TO PLAY KEYSTONE COP, GO DO IT SOMEWHERE ELSE WHERE IT WON'T KILL OUR BUZZ.

BLESSED IS THE LORD OUR GOD. RULER OF THE UNIVERSE. CREATOR OF THE FRUIT OF THE VINE.
LIFE IS SHORT. WE DO NOT HAVE LONG TO GLADDEN THE HEARTS THAT TRAVEL WITH US.
GOD, PLEASE GIVE ME THE STRENGTH TO REMAIN CALM AND CARRY ON.

EXCUSE ME, CAN YOU PLEASE BE QUIET? WE ARE TRYING TO PRAY.

RING
RING
RING

RING
RING

Seven

WILL YOU PLEASE BE QUIET? 'WE' ARE TRYING TO PRAY.

RING
RING
SWIPE

RING
RING
SWIPE

HeHeHe
He

ALRIGHT, BABY...
SAY HELLO TO THE
WHITE RABBIT.

HMM....

I THINK I SPOT A
PUSSY CAT. I DO! I DO!
A BIG RACIST PUSSYCAT.

Dad
DAD, I FOUND SOMETHING BIG!
KAIA!
IT'S HIS WIFE. JIM PICKET.
SHE WAS INVOLVED IN MOM'S MURDER.
WAFFLE HOUSE
THANK YOU FOR NOT SMOKING
KAIA?
296

KAIA, CAN YOU HEAR ME?
DAD! YOU HAVE TO LOOK AT THE PHONE.
WHAT?
TAKE THE PHONE AWAY FROM YOUR EAR AND LOOK AT IT.
OH, WOW. THAT'S YOU.
YEAH, IT'S FACETIME. LIKE I SHOWED YOU.
GIVE ME ONE SECOND...
...I'M JUST GOING TO FIND SOMEWHERE QUIET.
3B 2016

DID YOU HEAR ME?! IT'S JIM PICKET'S WIFE. SHE HAD SOMETHING TO DO WITH MOM'S MURDER.
HOW DO YOU KNOW ABOUT HIS WIFE? WHERE ARE YOU?
I NEED YOUR LOGIN TO THE EUREKA SPRINGS POLICE DEPARTMENT DATABASE.
WHAT?! ARE YOU CRAZY?
I COPIED ALL YOUR CASE FILES BEFORE YOU LEFT. I'M DOING MY OWN INVESTIGATION AND I'M FINDING VALUABLE STUFF. I CAN HELP YOU.
KAIA, LISTEN TO ME.
WE DON'T NEED COPS LIKE YOU ANYMORE. SOME ANTIQUATED PATRIARCHAL IDEA OF PROTECTING THE WEAK. MAYBE IT USED TO BE A JOB FOR SOME VERSION OF THE GOOD GUY. BUT THAT TIME HAS PASSED.
KAIA... YOU DON'T UNDERSTAND.

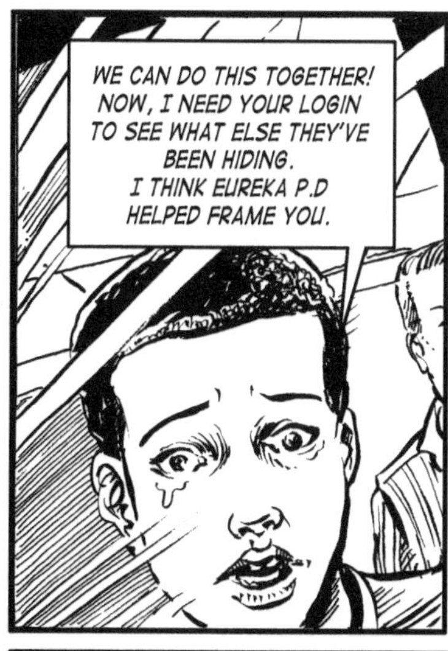

WE CAN DO THIS TOGETHER! NOW, I NEED YOUR LOGIN TO SEE WHAT ELSE THEY'VE BEEN HIDING. I THINK EUREKA P.D HELPED FRAME YOU.

THEY DIDN'T FRAME ME. YOU'RE TALKING LIKE A CHILD. THINKING YOU CAN TEAR DOWN ALL OF SOCIETY, AND REBUILD IT YOURSELF.

I FOUND A SERIOUS LEAD! YOU ALREADY MISSED THE CHANCE ONCE TO BE MY FATHER WHEN YOU LET THEM TAKE MY MOTHER. I DON'T WANT TO HAVE TO DO THIS ALONE TOO. PLEASE HELP ME!
I'M SORRY, KAIA.

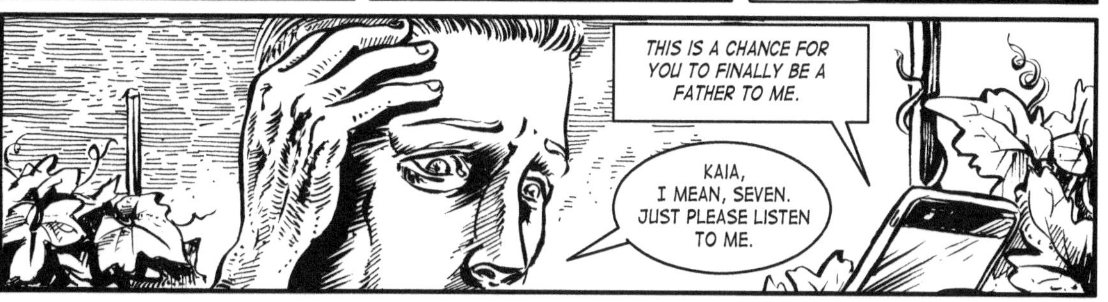

THIS IS A CHANCE FOR YOU TO FINALLY BE A FATHER TO ME.
KAIA, I MEAN, SEVEN. JUST PLEASE LISTEN TO ME.

GOODBYE, DAD.

GOLD MEDAL
IS THAT DRUGS YOU'RE PUTTING IN MY WINE?
DON'T WORRY, I WAS A CHEMIST BEFORE I WAS A COP.
LET'S GO, MY CI JUST SHOWED.
LET ME TAKE THE LEAD ON THIS.

STOP, THAT'S ENOUGH, I SAID.
JESUS...WHO IS THIS GUY?? I'M IN THE PROGRAM!

I WANT YOU TO TELL ME WHAT YOU KNOW ABOUT JIM PICKET.
YOU GOT IT ALL WRONG MAN.

HERE. HAVE ANOTHER DRINK.

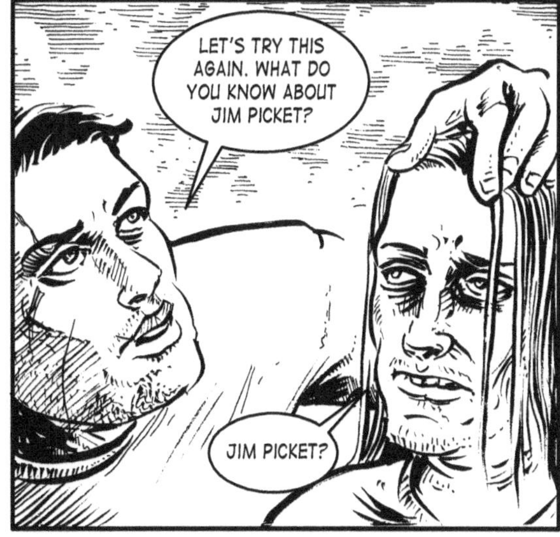

LET'S TRY THIS AGAIN. WHAT DO YOU KNOW ABOUT JIM PICKET?
JIM PICKET?

TELL US WHAT YOU KNOW ABOUT HEAVENLY FARMS.
I DON'T KNOW ABOUT PIG FARMS.
...I'M A VEGETARIAN, MAN.
YOU THINK YOU'RE FUNNY?
IT'S A LIE THAT THE MEN CONTROL EVERYTHING! IT'S THE BITCHES!
OH, REALLY? YOU HEAR THAT ON A PODCAST, PETEY?
I'M TRYING TO HELP YOU.
YOU COULDN'T HELP A WHORE WITH A HAND JOB.
WE'RE THE ONES BEING CONTROLLED, MAN! MY EYES ARE OPEN.

WHAT THE FUCK ARE YOU SAYING?

YOU KNOW HOW DANGEROUS THIS IS FOR ME?! I'M JUST TRYING TO KEEP MYSELF FROM GOING BACK TO JAIL. THAT'S WHY I'VE COME TO YOU WITH THIS!

NOBODY TOLD YOU TO GET YOUR DICK CAUGHT IN THAT ARKANSAS GATOR WHIP. HERE, HAVE ANOTHER DRINK.

I DON'T WANT ANYMORE WINE! CAN YOU JUST FUCKING LISTEN?!

FROM WHAT I CAN TELL, WE GOT YOUR COUSIN UP IN VARNER, GOT YOUR BROTHER QUESTIONING HIS SEXUALITY DOWN IN LEAVENWORTH. SHIT PETEY..,

...WE GOT YOUR MOM KNITTING QUILTS, SERVING 18 MONTHS IN WOMEN'S CORRECTIONAL. YOU WANNA TEST ME AND SEE HOW FAR THAT WHITE SUPREMACIST BULLSHIT GOES IN COUNTY, KNOCK YOURSELF OUT.

I CAME TO TELL YOU ABOUT HER!

AND WHO IS 'HER'? ENLIGHTEN US.
THE BITCHES MAN! THEY CONTROL OUR LIVES. THEY CONTROL OUR THOUGHTS. THEY CONTROL WHAT WE SAY AND DO! THEY CONTROL EVERYTHING.
ALT-RIGHT, PETEY? WHERE YOU GOING WITH THIS?
YOU'RE GONNA BE IN DEEP DOO DOO.
PETEY...FOCUS. THE WHITE LIONS ARE RUNNING CARRIER LINES UP AND DOWN THE WHOLE STATE. I GOT 'H' AS FAR AS TENNESSEE. BUT I KNOW THERE'S NO WAY THEY ARE BRINGING THIS SHIT UP FROM TEXAS WITHOUT THE CARTELS KNOWING... SO WHAT'S GOING ON?
All my exe's live in Texas
TELL US WHAT YOU KNOW ABOUT JIM PICKETT?
SOMETHING IS NOT RIGHT...THESE COLORS TASTE FUNNY.

PETEY...IF YOU AIN'T CAREFUL, YOU'RE GONNA TIP THE BOAT OVER.
THEY GOT PLENTY OF BOATS.
TUG BOATS. SHRIMPING BOATS. FISHING BOATS ALL THE WAY UP TO MISSISSIPPI. NOT EVEN YOU CAN TIP THAT BOAT.
WAIT, WHAT DID HE JUST SAY? WRITE THAT DOWN.
BRINGING IT UP THE MISSISSIPPI? FROM THE GULF! WHO IS?
Big Wheel Keep on turnin'
THE BOAR ISN'T REAL, MAN! IT'S A BIG GOVERNMENT CONSPIRACY TO REPLACE US WITH WOMEN!
Proud Mary Keep on burnin'
PETEY! LET'S JUST BREATHE. SLOW IT DOWN. WHOSE BOATS?
EVENTUALLY THEY'LL ONLY NEED US FOR OUR SPERM!
rollin'

THEY'LL KEEP US IN CAGES AND MILK US LIKE COWS!
rollin' rollin'
on the river...
IT WON'T BE AWESOME!
I SMELL DEMONS. I SHOULD HAVE KNOWN IT WAS YOU! YOU'RE THE ONE THEY SENT TO KILL THE ONE!
WHAT?
IT'S YOU! YOU'RE THE INSIDE MAN. YOU'RE THE BOAR. THE REASON THEY KILLED COLBA.
COLBA? WHAT DO YOU KNOW ABOUT MY PARTNER'S MURDER?
OINK OINK OINK

UCK YOU!
I TRUSTED YOU!
YOU WERE SUPPOSED
TO BE MY PROTECTOR,
YOU BITCH! I KNEW
I SHOULDN'T
TRUST WOMEN!
WHAT THE FUCK
WAS THAT?
I DON'T KNOW.
PERHAPS WE CAN'T
TRUST ANYTHING
HE SAYS.
YA THINK?
MAYBE IT WAS
A BAD IDEA TO SLIP
HIM THAT ACID.
YOU WHAT?!

I THOUGHT IT WOULD HELP. THE CIA USED TO USE IT TO PULL INFORMATION FROM SUSPECTS ALL THE TIME.
THIS ISN'T THE 1950'S! EVERYTHING HE JUST SAID WAS NONSENSE.
WHERE DID YOU GET IT?
I TOOK IT OFF THOSE WHITE LIONS. THE ONES THAT JUST RAN INTO THE FOREST.
IN WHAT WORLD DID YOU THINK THAT WAS OK?
THIS ONE?
HE SAID HE HAD VALUABLE INFORMATION ABOUT THE TRUE IDENTITY OF THE BOAR.

HE SAID WOMEN WILL MILK US ONE DAY LIKE COWS. HE WAS FUCKING CRAZY. PLUS WE ALREADY KNOW WHO THE BOAR IS. WE'RE RAIDING HIS HOUSE TOMORROW.
WHY WOULD YOU DO THIS?
I WANTED TO MAKE SURE HE WASN'T LYING.
EVERYTHING HE JUST SAID TO US, IS NOW INADMISSIBLE IN COURT.
I DON'T CARE ABOUT COURT... ...THEY SENT ME COLBA'S FINGERS AND TEETH. HIS FAMILY BURIED A BOX OF BRICKS. I'M GONNA KILL THEM ALL!
I AM SORRY YOU LOST YOUR PARTNER, BUT I CAN'T BE A PART OF THIS ANYMORE.
BUT I NEED YOU! THE JUDGE WON'T GIVE ME THE WARRANT WITHOUT YOU.
YOU'RE A TICKING TIME BOMB. AND NEITHER ME NOR ANYONE FROM MY DEPARTMENT IS GOING TO BE ANYWHERE NEAR YOU WHEN IT GOES OFF.

CHAPTER SEVEN
BIG TITS SINK SHIPS
or
the PROBLEM WITH BIBLICAL BARNACLES

GOD, PLEASE, GIVE ME A SIGN! WHAT DO I DO?

HEY, YOU LITTLE SLUT! GET BACK HERE!
EXCUSE ME?!
312

313

NO. PLEASE JUST STOP WHATEVER YOU ARE DOING. GO DO IT SOMEWHERE ELSE, PLEASE.
HEY, I REMEMBER YOU! DID YOU FOLLOW US HERE?
NO. I'M JUST. ...TRYING TO PRAY.
SURE BUDDY! YOU FUCKING PERVERT!
PUT ON YOUR CLOTHES AND PLEASE GO.
WE'RE NOT LEAVING! YOU LEAVE. WE WERE HERE FIRST.
I WAS HERE FIRST.
FINE! I'LL MAKE YOU LEAVE.

BABE, LET IT GO!
YOU GOTTA STAND YOUR GROUND...
THIS IS SOOO STUPID!
THIS, IS EXACTLY WHAT'S WRONG WITH THIS COUNTRY. THEY TAKE ONE INCH AT A TIME! NOT ON MY WATCH!
CRACK
CALM DOWN SIR.
315

THAT'S EXACTLY WHAT THAT ASSHOLE WHO STOLE OUR DRUGS SAID! WE AIN'T FALLING FOR THAT AGAIN!
I'M A POLICE OFFICER.
WHAT ARE YOU GONNA DO? SHOOT ME?!
SIR, PUT ON YOUR PANTS AND DROP THE WEAPON.

317

SPLAS
AAAHHH

LADY, WAIT...
...IT'S OKAY.
I REALLY AM
A COP!

NO! NO! NO! PLEASE DON'T KILL ME!
PLEASE, DON'T! I'LL DO ANYTHING!
GIVE ME THAT BIG BOY!
STOP IT. STOP! YOU DO NOT NEED TO DO THAT.

I AM NOT GOING TO KILL YOU.
CALM DOWN. NO ONE IS GOING TO DIE.
I DON'T WANT TO DIE!
I HAVE A DAUGHTER! SHE'S WITH MY PARENTS BUT I LOVE HER AND I WANT TO BE A GOOD MOM.
I HAVE A DAUGHTER, TOO.
IT'S OKAY.
YOU CAN'T HURT ME. I'M A WOMAN.
I DON'T PLAN ON HURTING YOU...I REALLY AM A COP. I WON'T ARREST YOU.

YOU KILLED HIM!!!
IT WAS AN ACCIDENT. YOU NEED TO COME WITH ME TO THE STATION AND EXPLAIN WHAT HAPPENED.
LADY, STOP RUNNING.
I'M ONLY TRYING TO HELP.

324

HEY, CRACKER JACK.
ARE YOU FUCKING KIDDING ME?
IT'S GOOD TO SEE YOU TOO, BYRON.

ARE YOU OUT OF YOUR FUCKING MIND? WHAT ARE YOU DOING HERE?
I'M SORRY, BABE.

YOU COULD BLOW EVERYTHING.

LISTEN...,

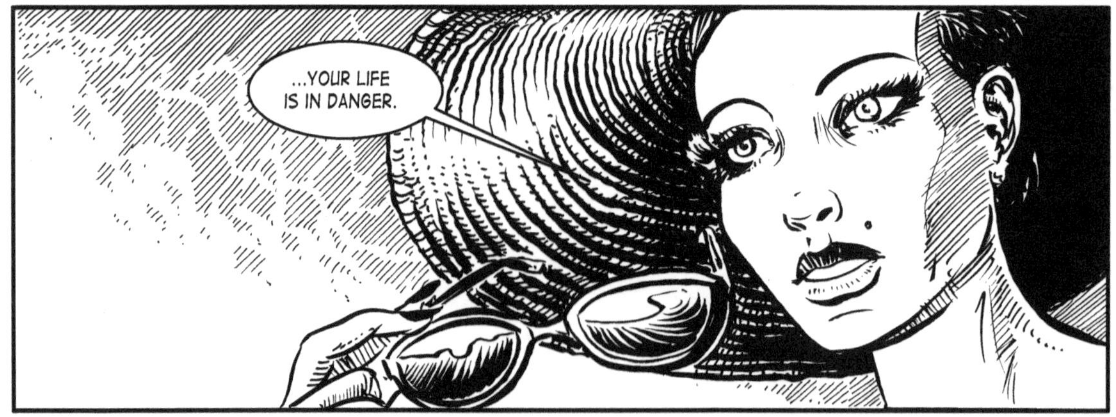

...YOUR LIFE IS IN DANGER.

OH, "MY LIFE IS IN DANGER" FUCK YOU!
SLIP

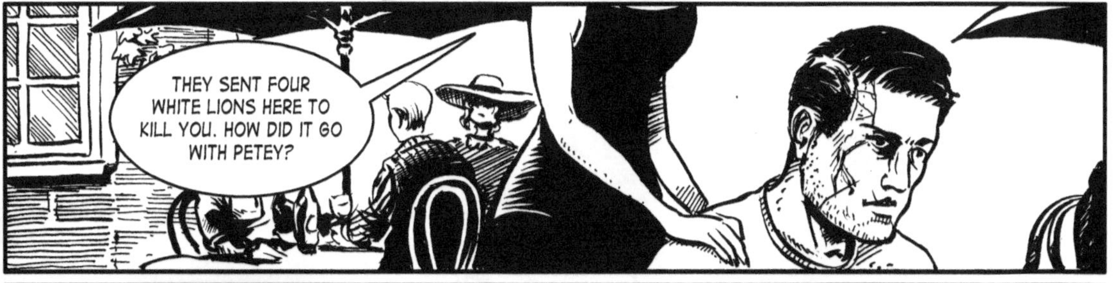

THEY SENT FOUR WHITE LIONS HERE TO KILL YOU. HOW DID IT GO WITH PETEY?

HE DIDN'T SAY ANYTHING. BUT WE HAVE A BIGGER PROBLEM NOW. SAMANTHA HAS BACKED OUT ON GETTING US THE WARRANT.
WHAT DID YOU DO?

I DID WHAT I HAD TO DO TO KEEP PETEY QUIET.

I TOLD YOU NOT TO WORRY ABOUT HIM. HE'S A NOBODY.

FOR A NOBODY HE SURE SEEMED TO KNOW A LOT.
YOU LET THEM KILL COLBA. HOW CAN I EVER TRUST YOU AGAIN?
CHOICES HAD TO BE MADE TO SAVE MY LIFE AND YOURS. I'M NOT SORRY FOR IT. I CAN'T ALWAYS CONTROL THEM. YOU KNOW I LOVE YOU, BABE. I'M SORRY.
I DON'T THINK YOUR'E CAPABLE OF LOVE. I THINK YOU MIGHT BE ONE OF THOSE LIZARD PEOPLE.
LET'S PRETEND THAT'S TRUE. THAT I'M NOT HERE TO MAKE THINGS RIGHT OR APOLOGIZE. I'M AT LEAST HERE TRYING TO SAVE YOUR LIFE.
328

MEET ME AT THE TRAIN STATION AT 7. WE WON'T HAVE ANOTHER CHANCE.
NO. FUCK YOU! I DON'T WANT ANYTHING TO DO WITH YOU OR YOUR NAZI FRIENDS. YOU WERE A FUCKING MISTAKE.
I'M ALREADY DOING EVERYTHING I CAN TO KEEP THE LIONS FROM KILLING YOU. DON'T MAKE THIS ANY HARDER THAN IT IS.
PRIDE

WHAT DO I DO?
I CAN'T GO BACK
TO PRISON!

...I CAN'T LEAVE HER AGAIN.

Spring
Gorge
Crystal
Falls
Gorge
Road
Spring
Gorge
Crystal
Falls

332

Pride

Pride

Pride

BIP
BIP

Puff
Puff

CALM.
TRY TO STAY CALM.
IS THIS WHISKEY?

FUCK IT.
IT WILL HELP TAKE
THE EDGE OFF.

EDEN VALLEY VINEYARD
cellar door
tastings
restaurant

BYRON?... BYRON? CAN I PLEASE HAVE THE CAR KEYS?
I LITERALLY JUST GAVE THEM TO YOU. WHY ARE YOU STILL STANDING THERE? WHAT'S WRONG WITH YOU?
I THINK I ATE SOMETHING BAD. I'LL MEET YOU AT THE HOUSE.

Chapter Eight

One Hour Later

Was There ACID in That Whiskey?

WHAT FEELS LIKE MANY HOURS LATER...

utensils
345

DENTAL

351

DADDY!
LOOK AT WHAT ME AND MOMMY FOUND
OH, HEY! A LITTLE LADY BUG.

OFF SHE GOES.
BUT I WANTED TO KEEP HER AS A PET!
DON'T BE SAD, SHE'S PROBABLY FLYING HOME TO HER OWN MOMMY AND DADDY.
MAYBE SHE'LL TELL THEM ABOUT THE BIG GIANT SHE MET TODAY.
DON'T BE SO SILLY DADDY! I'M NOT A BIG GIANT!
NO, OF COURSE YOU'RE NOT, YOU'RE MY LITTLE PRINCESS.

MEANWHILE...
INFORMATION
3A
OH, NANA!
WE'LL GET YOU OUT OF HERE SOON AS WE CAN.

DID I DREAM YOUR DAD IS BACK?
YOU REMEMBER DAD?
RING! RING!
WAIT... IT'S HIM.
RING! RING!
DAD?
KAIA!
WHAT'S WRONG?

I JUST NEEDED
TO TALK TO MY LITTLE
PRINCESS.

WHAT'S WRONG WITH YOU?
YOU DON'T SOUND WELL. LOOK, I WANTED TO APOLOGIZE...
NO! YOU'RE RIGHT ABOUT EVERYTHING! YOU'RE ALL THAT MATTERS NOW! YOU AND I NEED TO SOLVE THIS CASE TOGETHER!
I SEE HIM NOW. JESUS TOLD ME FROM HIS DINOSAUR. FAMILY IS ALL THAT MATTERS.
DAD! WHAT'S HAPPENING?!
WHAT?! ... ARE YOU ON DRUGS?
YOU'RE ON YOUR OWN.
MY PASSWORD IS... KAIALADYBUG1996

DAD! WHO GAVE YOU DRUGS?!
358

OH MY GOD! NO!
I'M ON DRUGS!

DAD, DAD!
KAIA! IS THAT YOU?
I CAN'T SEE YOU! WHERE ARE YOU?! I HAVE THE PASSWORD. IT'S...
KAIALADYBUG1996
DAD! WHAT IS HAPPENING?

I LOVE YOU!
I'M SORRY.
IF I DON'T SEE YOU AGAIN.
I'M SO SORRY FOR EVERYTHING!
I LOVE YOU!
WHAT DO YOU MEAN, NOT SEE ME AGAIN?!
THE PHONE NEEDS TO DIE!
CRACK
DAD?
DAD!
DAD!!
DAD!!!

IS YOUR FATHER OKAY?
I DON'T THINK SO...
BUT I GOT HIS POLICE LOGIN.
EUREKA SPRINGS POLICE DEPARTMENT
MEMBER LOGIN
USERNAME   ALPALMER
PASSWORD   KAIALADYBUG1996
SIGN IN
SEARCH: LORETTA PICKET
5'6" 5' 4'6" 4' 3'6" 3' 2'6"
LORETTA PICKET:
MULTIPLE ARRESTS FOR   - ASSAULT
                        - DRUG TRAFFICKING
                        - DRUNK DRIVING
CRIMINAL HISTORY REMOVED FROM OFFICIAL RECORD
IN EXCHANGE FOR ONGOING SUPPLY OF INFORMATION
HOLY SHIT!
LORETTA PICKET: PAID INFORMANT.
OFFICER NOTES: HAS CONSISTENTLY GIVEN
RELIABLE INTEL ON THE TRUE IDENTITY AND
BUSINESS DEALING OF HER HUSBAND, AKA "THE
BOAR." BELIEVES HUSBAND "THE BOAR" IS A
PROTECTED CIA ASSET.

I KNEW YOU'D COME.
WHAT AM I DOING HERE, LO?
HERE.
WHAT THE ACTUAL FUCK?
THAT'S COLBA'S SHARE.
GIVE IT TO HIS FAMILY OR WHATEVER...
I WASN'T BEING GREEDY... IT JUST HAD TO BE DONE.
RAIL PASS

LAST TIME I SAW YOU WE WERE ARGUING OVER A $30 GAS BILL...

CAN I STILL COUNT ON YOU TO MAKE THE ARREST?

SURE THING, BABE.

YOU HAVE THE RIGHT TO REMAIN SILENT...

BYRON, DON'T BE STUPID! I COULDN'T HELP HIM.

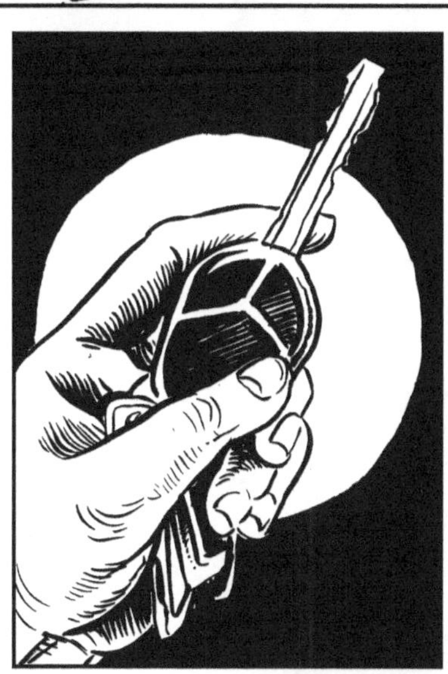

EVERYTHING YOU SAY OR DO WILL BE USED AGAINST YOU...
THEY'LL FUCKING KILL YOU!

K'TCK
THEY'LL FEED YOU TO THE FUCKING PIGS!

RELAX BACK THERE, BABE..
YOU'RE GOING TO HURT YOURSELF.

YOU'LL GO TO JAIL TOO! I'LL TAKE YOU DOWN WITH ME.

HE SAID, SHE SAID.

YOU AND ME! WE GO TO THE BAHAMAS AND DISAPPEAR LIKE WE PLANNED TO!

I'M NOT GOING TO THE BAHAMAS WITH YOU...
...YOU FUCKING NAZI.

IT WASN'T MY FAULT. BUT I HAVE A PLAN. WE CAN GET THEM BACK TOGETHER.
THE PLAN IS FUCKED. SAMANTHA IS CALLING OFF THE RAID. WITH NO WARRANT THERE'S NOTHING WE CAN DO ABOUT "JIM PICKET."

I PROMISE YOU, WE'LL FIGURE SOMETHING OUT.
HOT SPRINGS
POLICE DEPARTMENT

I WAS THE ONE WHO TOLD YOU WHAT REALLY HAPPENED TO COLBA, REMEMBER?
I COULD HAVE LIED TO YOU BUT I TOLD YOU THE TRUTH BECAUSE YOU DESERVED TO KNOW.
BECAUSE I STILL CARE ABOUT YOU.

HE WAS MY FRIEND TOO, YOU KNOW?
WE'LL GET OUR REVENGE TOGETHER.

YOU BELONG IN PRISON.

IF I BELONG IN PRISON, THEN YOU DO TOO.

I GUESS WE'LL HAVE TO LET A JURY DECIDE...
I STILL HAVE THE DRESS.

"HE SAID, SHE SAID." I WONDER WHOSE DNA IS ON THAT?

YOU AND ME CAN STILL SURVIVE THIS. THEY DON'T WANT US. THEY WANT PALMER.

OH, SHIT. PALMER, HE'S AT THE HOUSE.

MEANWHILE...

TAP
TAP

376

377
TAP
TAP

TAP
THUD
TAP
TAP
OH MY GOD!
TAP TAP
THUD
EVROLET
THEY'RE STILL ALIVE!

THUD
TAP

YOU SEND
THOSE MEN?!

HE KNOWS
TOO MUCH.

I HOPE YOU'RE
INSURED FOR MORE
THAN THOSE TITTIES.

NO! I JUST
GOT THIS CAR!

CRASH!

SCREEE
WHITE PRIDE
384

SCREE

CLICK

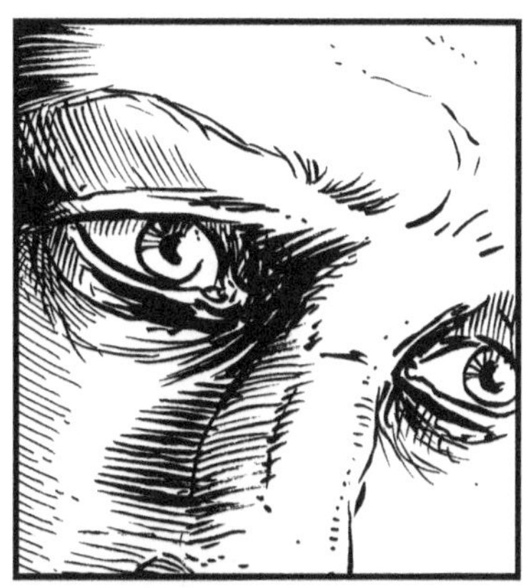

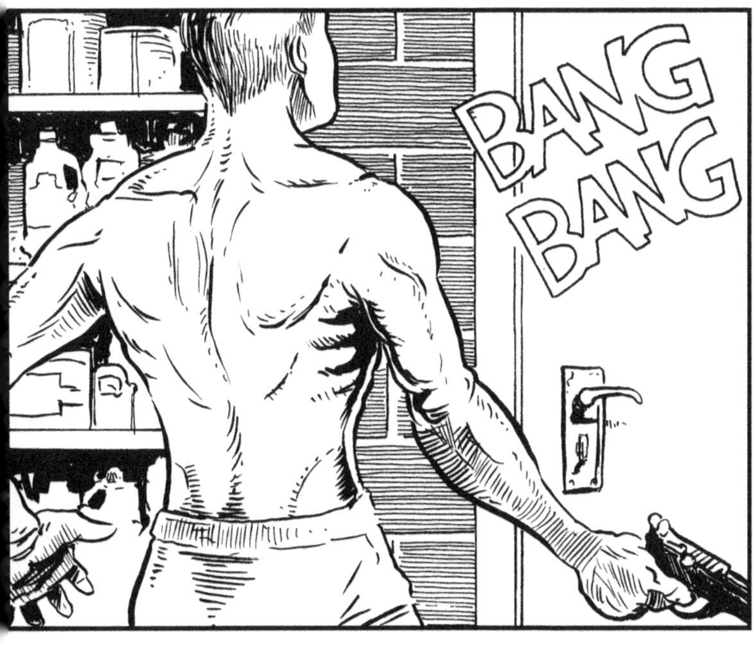

BANG
BANG

IT'S NOT REAL. IT'S NOT REAL. IT'S ALL IN YOUR HEAD. YOU'RE SAFE.
THAT'S NOT GONNA STOP THEM.
BANG BANG
WHAT DID YOU SAY?
YOU BETTER DO SOMETHING.
JIGGLE
JIGGLE
THE DEAD ARE NOT REAL.

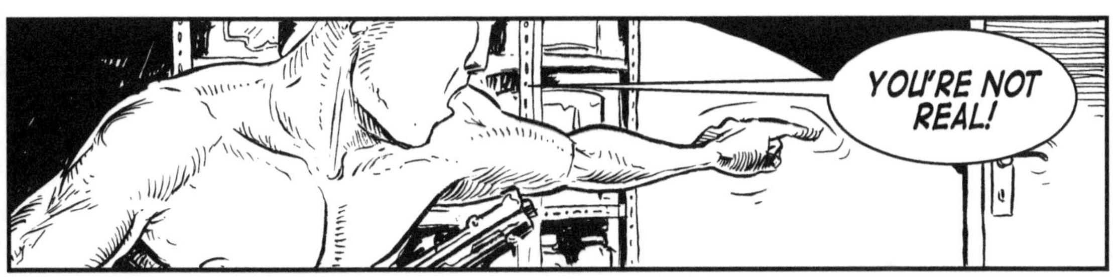

YOU'RE NOT REAL!

YOU HAVE TO DEFEND YOURSELF.

YOU AREN'T REAL! SHUT UP!

IT'S KILL OR BE KILLED...
THAT'S MOTHER NATURE.

390

BAM
BAM
BAM
BAM
BAM
BAM

Al! Is that you? They are here to KILL YOU!!!
HERE. USE THIS.

PALMER! LET
ME IN!

MORE ARE
COMING.

We Have
to Go
NONE OF THIS
IS REAL!

YOU'LL HAVE TO
MAKE A CHOICE.

395

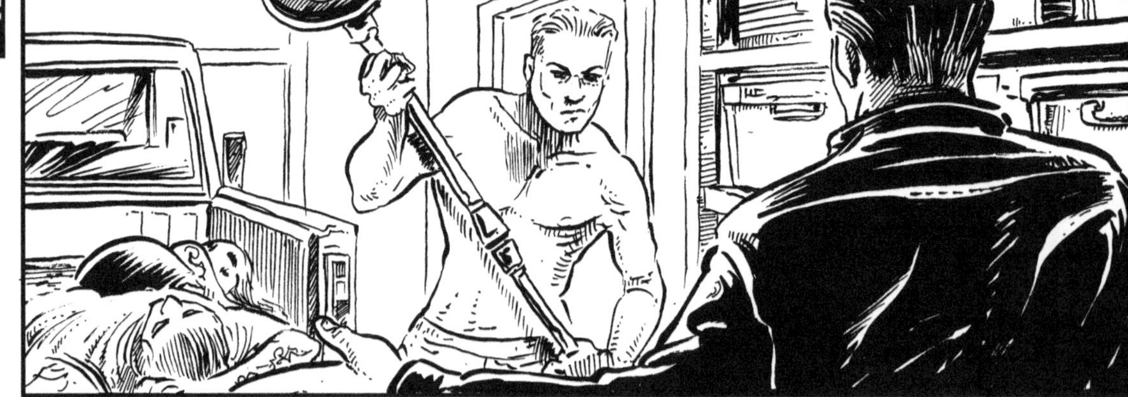

WHAT THE
ACTUAL FUCK?

Huff Huff
Huff

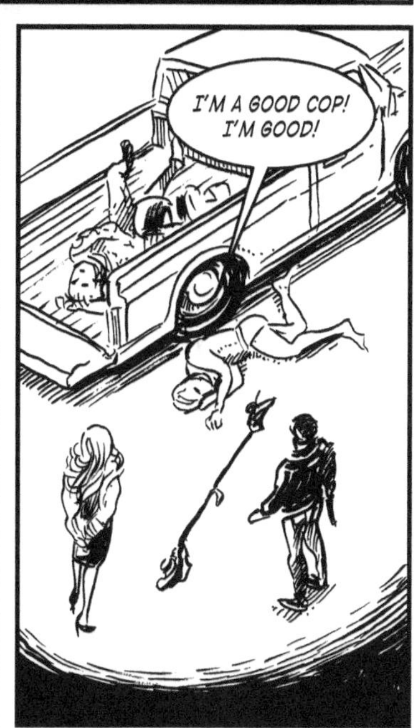

I'M A GOOD COP!
I'M GOOD!

WAIT!
HE'S A COP.

WHAT ABOUT
HIM?

...WILL A JUDGE ISSUE HIM A WARRANT?

CHAPTER NINE

The BOAR

A FEW HOURS LATER...
WE'RE NOT GONNA BEAT THE SUN!
I THINK WE SHOULD WAKE HIM UP.
YOU'RE THE ONE THAT WANTED TO LET HIM SLEEP AND DIG FOUR SEPARATE GRAVES.
THEY WERE FOUR DIFFERENT PEOPLE. THEY SHOULD HAVE THEIR OWN GRAVE.
I'M JUST SAYING WE COULD HAVE DONE IT QUICKER.

HEY!

OH, GOOD, YOU'RE AWAKE.
YOU CAN HELP US DIG. THERE'S A SHOVEL AT YOUR FEET.

WHAT'S GOING ON?
WE'RE BURYING THE PEOPLE WE KILLED.
GET UP AND HELP US WITH YOUR HALF.

IT'S NOT WHAT YOU THINK. I DIDN'T MEAN TO KILL THEM!

IT WAS AN ACCIDENT! *I SWEAR TO GOD!* HE CAME AT ME WITH A STICK.
I DIDN'T KILL MY WIFE!

WE KNOW. RELAX.
YOU DID THE WORLD A FAVOR.
THESE RACIST ASSHOLES ARE IN WHITE SUPREMACIST HEAVEN.

THEY'RE NOT RACIST. THEY JUST THINK THEY HAVE A RIGHT TO BE PROUD OF THEIR HERITAGE.

YIKES! YOU HEAR THAT? THEY'RE JUST "PROUD" OF THEIR HERITAGE OF OWNING PEOPLE.

WHAT'S GOING ON?!

CHIEF WHITE TRIED TO HAVE YOU KILLED. SHE TRIED TO HELP.
WHAT?

POLICE CHIEF WHITE FOUND OUT THEY WERE TESTING THE NEW EVIDENCE...,
...HE WAS RESPONSIBLE FOR THE HACK THAT GOT YOU TRANSFERRED TO GEN-POP SO THE WHITE LIONS COULD KILL YOU.
THAT FAILED, SO HE SET IT UP SO THAT YOU WOULD DIE DOWN HERE WITH ME.

NO! NO!
HE SENT YOU HERE TO SPY ON ME?
THINKS I'M "WORKING WITH THE WHITE LIONS?"

ASK YOURSELF THIS, WHAT WERE YOU DOING RIGHT BEFORE YOUR WIFE WAS MURDERED? RIGHT BEFORE THEY SENT YOU TO PRISON?

INVESTIGATING JIM PICKET AND THE WHITE LIONS...

THE CHIEF TOLD ME TO DROP IT BUT I WOULDN'T LISTEN.

KAIA, WAS RIGHT...
I NEVER SHOULD HAVE TRUSTED THEM.

THE CHIEF KILLED MY WIFE?

HE'S BEEN WORKING WITH JIM PICKET FOR YEARS.
AKA THE FUCKING "BOAR"

I DIDN'T WANT TO HAVE TO KILL YOU. I WAS ACTUALLY TRYING TO HELP STOP THEM.
BUT BYRON FUCKED IT!

SHE'S A LIAR. SHE CONVINCED COLBA TO BETRAY ME. SHE ONLY PRETENDED LIKE SHE WANTED OUT.
I DID WANT OUT!!

HE OWNS THE BOATS... THE SHRIMPING BOATS, THE FISHING BOATS, THAT THEY USE TO BRING THE DRUGS UP THE MISSISSIPPI FROM MEXICO.
YOU KNOW, HEAVENLY FARMS? THE LARGEST PRODUCER OF PORK IN THE SOUTH? THEY USE HIS SLAUGHTERHOUSES AS A DISTRIBUTION NETWORK.

YOUR HUSBAND, IS THE BOAR?
I NEEDED MONEY. OKAY? HE HELPED ME. HE WAS NICE AT FIRST.
AND I DID WANT OUT! I HAD A GREAT PLAN...BUT BYRON FUCKED IT UP.
I'M SORRY I TRIED TO KILL YOU.

WHY DID THEY KILL MY WIFE?

TELL HIM.

TELL HIM! OR WE'RE GOING TO DIG A FIFTH GRAVE AND PUT YOU IN IT.

YOU WERE SUPPOSED TO BE ALONE.
THEY COULDN'T GET TO YOU SO THEY FOUND SOME DRUNK AT THE CLUB...,
...KILLED HIM AND DRAGGED HIM TO YOUR HOUSE...,
...PUT HIM IN THE BED WITH HER.

MY WIFE WASN'T CHEATING ON ME?
IT'S WHY THE DNA DIDN'T MATCH.
EVEN THOUGH WHITE DID EVERYTHING HE COULD TO TRY AND MAKE IT LOOK LIKE IT DID.

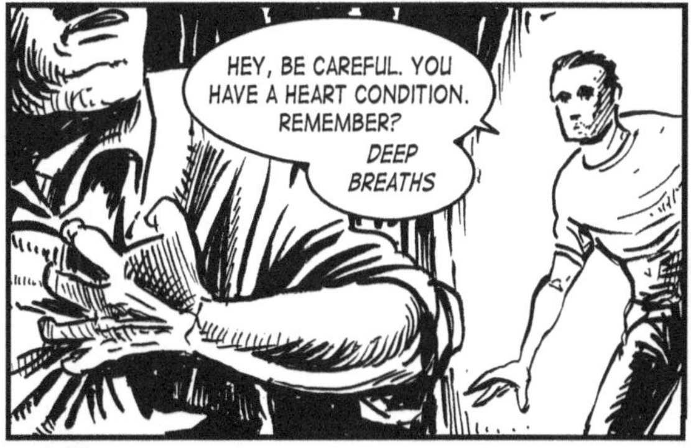

HEY, BE CAREFUL. YOU HAVE A HEART CONDITION. REMEMBER?
DEEP BREATHS

IT'S OKAY. WE HAVE A PLAN.

SAMANTHA WON'T GET US THE WARRANTS WE NEED BUT WITH YOUR RECENT PROMOTION....

INNOCENCE PROJECT LAW OFFICES
HEY SAM!
OH, NO...
YOU TWO COME TO FINISH THE JOB?
NANA WANTED TO SAY SORRY.
SORRY, FOR WHAT?
WAS THIS YOUR DAD'S PLAN ALL ALONG?
HE STILL VERY MUCH THINKS OF HIMSELF AS A COP. I DON'T THINK HE MEANT TO GIVE IT ME.
I NEED YOUR HELP DECIPHERING MY MOM'S CASE.
AFTER WE'RE DONE YOU CAN KEEP THE DRIVE. USE IT TO HELP WITH YOUR OTHER CASES.
I GOT MY DAD'S LOGIN TO THE EUREKA POLICE DEPARTMENT DATABASE. I STOLE ALL OF THEIR FILES AND PUT THEM ON THIS DRIVE.
IS HE RECONSIDERING SUING THE DEPARTMENT?

406

LATER THAT DAY...
GOVERNOR JIM PICKET IS THE BOAR.
THIS BETTER NOT BE PARTISAN.
I'VE BEEN A LIFELONG REPUBLICAN, SIR. IT BREAKS MY HEART WHAT HE'S DONE TO THE PARTY.
HOT SPRINGS MAGISTRATE COURT
Authorizing by Magistrate
Date:
No
ARREST WARRANT
HOT SPRINGS MAGISTRATES COURT
I NEED TO FIND A PHONE TO CALL MY DAUGHTER.
GOOD JOB CONVINCING THE JUDGE.
JIM PICKET for GOVERNOR
CHEVROLET

YOU NEED TO TAKE THIS TO CHIEF WHITE.
LORETTA PICKET: PAID INFORMANT.
MULTIPLE ARRESTS FOR
- ASSAULT
- DRUG TRAFFICKING
- DRUNK DRIVING
CRIMINAL HISTORY
REMOVED FROM
OFFICIAL RECORD
IN EXCHANGE FOR
ONGOING SUPPLY OF
5'
4'6"
4'
3'6"
3'
BUT HE SHOULD ALREADY KNOW THIS.
HUH? THAT'S ALARMING.
BRRR BRRR
HMM, UNKNOWN NUMBER...
BRRR
BRRR
FOOD and DRINK
HELLO?
2
DAD!
KAIA!

DAD? ARE YOU OKAY?!
WHAT HAPPENED LAST NIGHT?

EVERYTHING IS FINE.

MOM WASN'T CHEATING ON YOU! THE WOMAN I FOUND, SHE'S BEEN CONNECTED TO JIM PICKET THE ENTIRE TIME...
...SHE AND THESE TWO MEN FROM THE PINK GOAT FRAMED YOU!

LORETTA? I KNOW...SHE CONFESSED TO EVERYTHING. SHE'S GONNA HELP US TAKE DOWN HER HUSBAND.
WHAT?!

HOT SPRINGS P.D. AND I HAVE IT UNDER CONTROL. CHIEF WHITE IS DIRTY. WE HAVE A PLAN TO BRING THEM ALL DOWN.

DAD! WAIT! YOU CAN'T TRUST HER.
DON'T DO ANYTHING THIS WOMAN WANTS YOU TO DO. YOU SHOULD TALK TO GEORGE!

CHIEF WHITE IS DIRTY!

JUST LISTEN TO ME. YOU'RE MAKING A MISTAKE! YOU NEED TO STOP AND THINK. AT LEAST RUN THIS BY GEORGE.

NK
KAIA, DON'T TELL CHIEF WHITE ANYTHING. WE'LL TAKE JIM PICKET INTO CUSTODY TONIGHT... I GOT TO GO. I LOVE YOU.

WHAT WAS THAT ABOUT?
MY DAUGHTER FOUND OUT ABOUT LORETTA. SAYS SHE AND THESE TWO MEN FROM THE PINK GOAT HELPED LO FRAME ME.
YOU THINK IT WAS MARSHALL AND WHITE?
I DON'T KNOW. I'M WORRIED SHE'S GOING TO GO TO CHIEF WHITE LIKE I DID.
I HAVE A BAD FEELING ABOUT THIS. MAYBE WE SHOULD HOLD OFF. I DON'T TRUST LORETTA EITHER. I KNOW SHE'S LYING TO US ABOUT SOMETHING.
NO. THIS HAPPENS TONIGHT! JIM PICKET IS GOING DOWN!
WE TAKE HIM INTO CUSTODY AND THEN WE SORT THINGS OUT.
FOOD and DR
2

WHAT DO WE DO? MAYBE WHITE DID KILL MY MOM?

IT COULDN'T HAVE BEEN GEORGE.

NANA, WHAT DO KNOW ABOUT GEORGE?

HE'S FAMILY. HE NEVER DID STOP LOVING US.

RING RING
Kaia (Seven) mobile
GEORGE! IT'S SEVEN!
I'M SORRY, SEVEN. BUT YOU KNOW I PREFER TO BE ADDRESSED AS POLICE CHIEF WHITE.
THAT IS MY PREFERRED PRONOUN.
HE, HE, HE
I'M NOT IN THE MOOD, GEORGE!
BACK AT THE STATION, US BOYS CALL THAT A MICRO AGGRESSION. HE, HE, HE
GEORGE!
TRIGGERED! TRIGGERED. I'M FEELING VERY TRIGGERED.
I NEED TO HANG UP NOW, AND GO FIND A SAFE SPACE, WHERE PEOPLE WILL ADDRESS ME AS CHIEF.
HE, HE, HE

LISTEN CHIEF, MY DAD DOESN'T TRUST YOU ANYMORE. I THINK HE'S ABOUT TO DO SOMETHING STUPID.

...THIS WOMAN LORETTA PICKETT IS SUPPOSEDLY A POLICE INFORMANT, BUT I THINK SHE HELPED KILL MY MOM. SHE'S A LIAR.

HOW DO YOU KNOW ABOUT LORETTA? DID YOUR DAD TELL YOU THAT?

I NEED TO COME SEE YOU. SHARE WHAT I FOUND WITH YOU.
I'M ON MY WAY TO THE STATION NOW. MEET ME THERE IN FIFTEEN.

OKAY. I'LL MEET YOU THERE....BUT FIRST, ARE YOU MY GRANDFATHER?

I DON'T KNOW WHAT NORMA TOLD YOU. BUT... I'M SORRY SEVEN... SHE DIDN'T... IT'S COMPLICATED...
LET'S TALK IN PERSON.

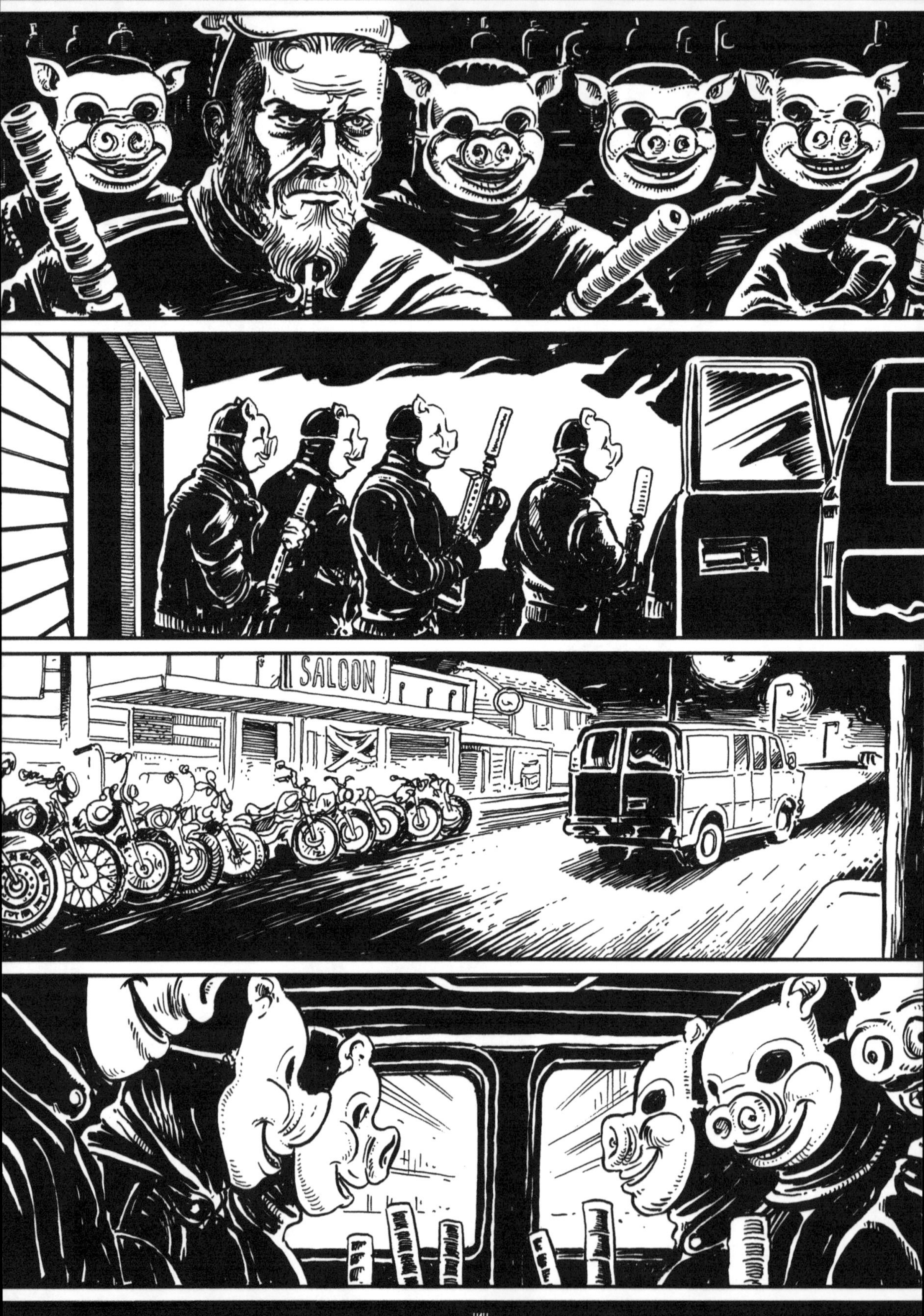
SALOON

SEVEN WILL BE HERE SOON. I THINK BYRON MIGHT HAVE FLIPPED PALMER.
WHAT DID HOT SPRINGS SAY?
GIVING US THE FUCKING RUN AROUND.
THEY SAID THEY CAN'T TRUST OUR DEPARTMENT. THAT THEY ARE KEEPING EVERYTHING IN-HOUSE.
GEEZE! WHAT THE HELL HAS HAPPENED TO US?
IT'S GOING TO BE OKAY, BUDDY. DON'T WORRY.
CUTE...

YOU DIDN'T SEE ME STANDING HERE, DID YOU?
THE WHITE MAN IS INVISIBLE THESE DAYS.
416

KLAK
KLAK
KLAK
KLAK
KLAK
KLAK
KLAK
417

POLICE
CHIEF
KLAK

RING
RING
RING
RING
RING
RING
420

RING RING
WELL, I'LL BE DAMNED.
LOOKS LIKE WE GOT TWO FOR THE PRICE OF ONE.
HAHAHAHA!

421

MEANWHILE...
SIR, WE HAVE A PROBLEM. IT'S THE EUREKA SPRINGS POLICE DEPARTMENT...
WHAT?!
THEY'RE ALL DEAD. MASSACRED. EXCEPT FOR CHIEF WHITE. HE'S MISSING.
WHAT DOES THAT HAVE TO DO WITH ME?
THEY WERE LEADING A CRIMINAL INVESTIGATION AGAINST YOU. IT DOESN'T LOOK GOOD. YOU SHOULD MAKE A STATEMENT CONDEMNING THIS. YOU NEED TO SEEM SAD.
DRAFT IT. BUT MAKE IT QUICK...,
...I'M SUPPOSED TO MEET MY WIFE IN AN HOUR.

CHAPTER
TEN

This is the
SHOOT
OUT

LATER THAT NIGHT...
POLICE
WHAT IF CHRIST WAS ONLY A MAN?
WHAT IF HE SUFFERED, AND DIED...AND THAT WAS IT?
NO RESURRECTION? NO REDEMPTION?
JUST NOTHING.
POLICE

I MEAN, THAT'S TECHNICALLY WHAT MOST OF THE WORLD ALREADY BELIEVES... BUT DON'T LOSE FAITH NOW.

LOOK WHO IT IS! I THOUGHT THE NEXT TIME I'D SEE YOU WOULD BE ON A CONJUGAL.

THE NIGHT IS STILL YOUNG. GLAD YOU COULD MAKE IT.
I'M DUMBER THAN I THOUGHT.
ICE
ALRIGHT, HERE'S THE PLAN...
DID I JUST HEAR YOU SAY PLAN? MR. "PLANS ARE FOR ARCHITECTS?"
POLICE
POLICE
SWA
SWA

426

POLICE
POLICE
POLICE

POLIC

SWAT
SWAT

PO

432

WHITE

PRIDE

DAKKA DAKKA
POW
POW
Batch 35c
Batch 35b
DAKKA
DAKKA
DAKKA
SWAT
436

PRIDE
BOOM
POLICE
POLICE

POLICE

RATTA
RATTA
Batch 326.
Batch 326.
COUGH
COUGH
441

DOFF
DOFF

DOFF
DOFF

OH, NO! PLEASE STOP!
DOFF
DOFF
DOFF

NO! NO! NO!

SHUT UP, BITCH! YOU FUCKING CUNT!
DOFF
DOFF

CRAKK
YOU KNOW YOU WANT IT!

442

HELP! HELP!
HE'S GOING TO
KILL ME!

YEAH, I'LL
FUCKING
KILL YOU!

DOFF
DOFF
DOFF

POL

DROP THE WEAPON!

HUH?

WHO THE FUCK
ARE YOU! WHAT
ARE YOU DOING
IN MY HOUSE?

DROP THE GUN NOW!!!

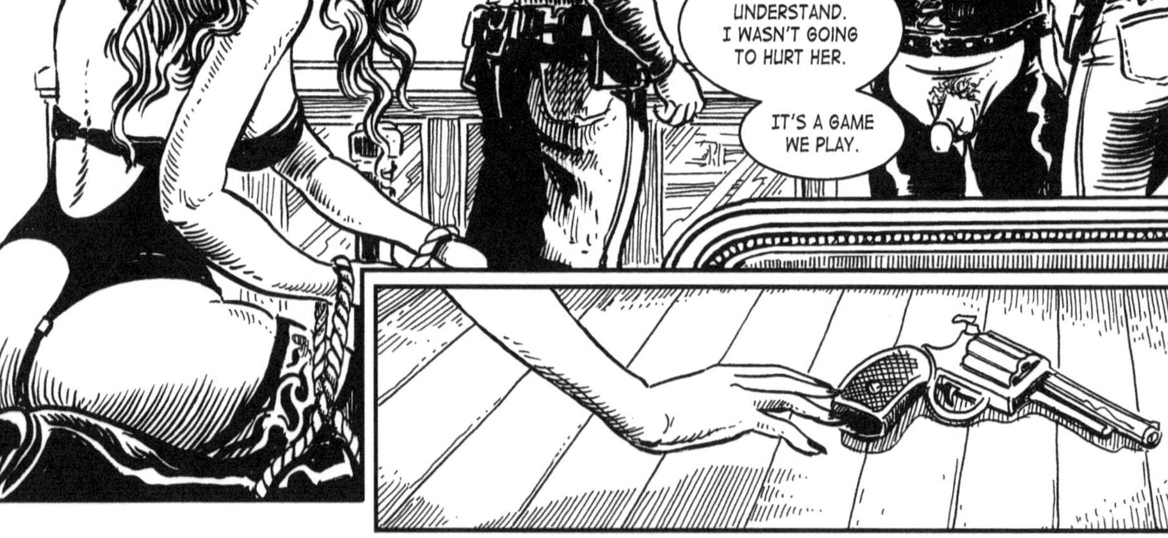

DROP IT, CRYING GAME, OR WE SHOOT!
DO YOU KNOW WHO I AM?
I SAID DROP IT!
FUCK YOU, YOU LITTLE SHIT!
IT'S NOT EVEN LOADED.
WE'RE JUST FOOLING AROUND!
GET ON YOUR KNEES! PUT YOUR HANDS ABOVE YOUR HEAD.
YOU DON'T UNDERSTAND. I WASN'T GOING TO HURT HER.
IT'S A GAME WE PLAY.
POLICE
POL

SAVE IT, YA FUCKING SICKO! NOW, GET ON YOUR KNEES. DON'T MAKE ME SHOOT YOU.
IT'S NOT WHAT IT LOOKS LIKE. WE JUST LIKE TO PLAY AROUND.
... THE GUN ISN'T EVEN LOADED.
FUCK YOU! YOU MONSTER! YOU'LL NEVER HURT ME AGAIN.
BANG
445

DROP THE GUN!
SORRY!
HE WAS GONNA KILL ME!
POLICE
I WAS SO SCARED!!!

COUGH COUGH
OH MY GOD, HOW COULD I BE SO STUPID?
Batch 36
PRIDE
POLICE

POLICE
VALUE

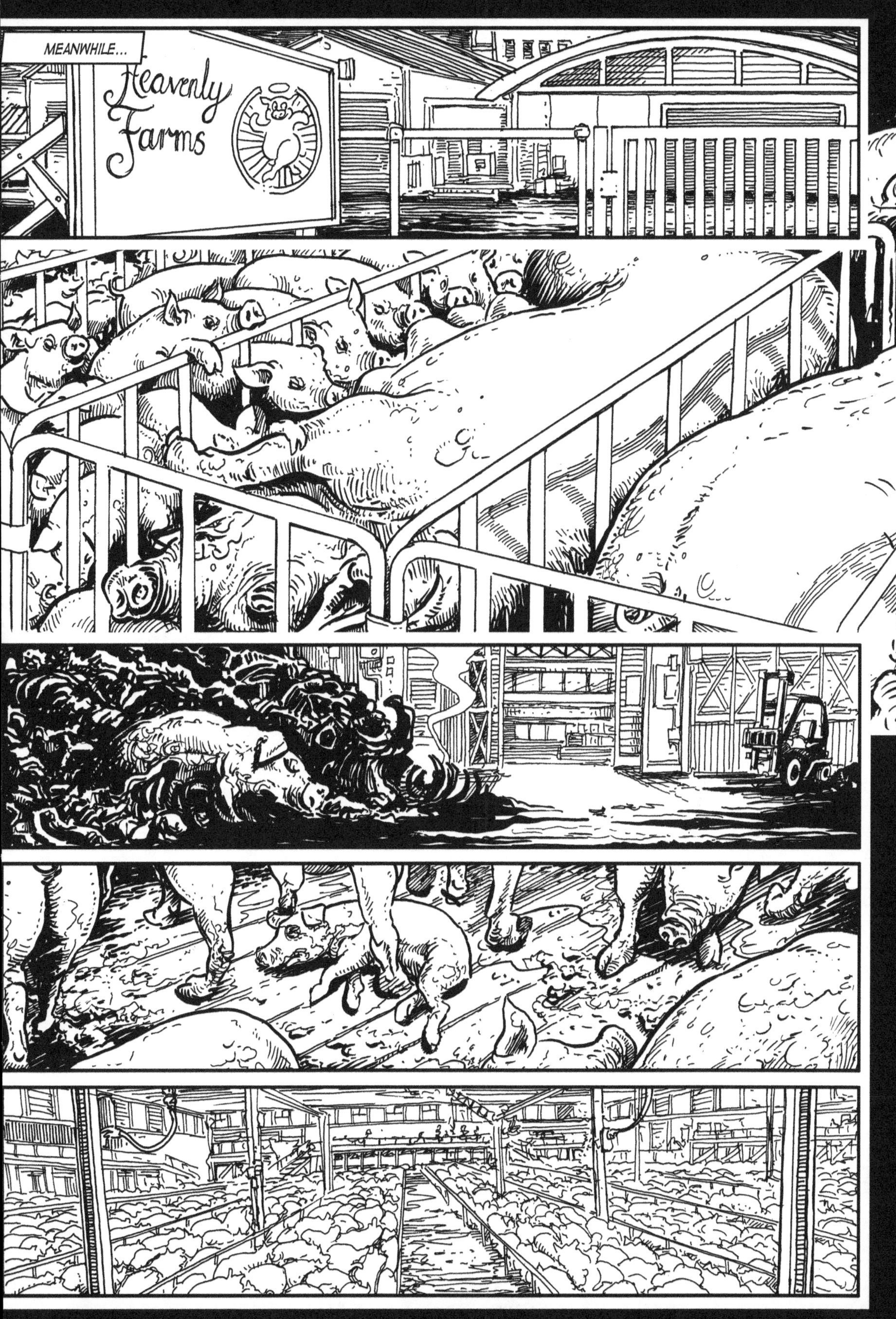
MEANWHILE...
Heavenly Farms

WHITE
450

MILK HELPS TO GREASE THE MOTORS.
THESE LITTLE FUCKERS WILL EAT ANYTHING.

451

RAG AND BONE.
'TIL NOTHING IS
LEFT.
JUST GIVE 'EM AN
OPPORTUNITY AND NO
ONE WILL EVER KNOW
YOU WALKED ON GOD'S
GREEN EARTH.
WHITE

OH, MY GOD.
YOU POOR THING.

LOOK, WHAT THAT MONSTER DID TO YOU.
PO

WHAT'S GOING ON UP HERE?
POLI

THIS WAS ALL A SHOW FOR US.
I KILLED HIM IN SELF DEFENSE!
I HAD TO! HE WAS GOING TO KILL ME!
POLICE
POLICE

OH GOD, WHAT HAVE I DONE?
PALMER!
PALMER! THEY HAVE YOUR DAUGHTER?!

455

MY DAUGHTER?!

CHIEF WHITE TOOK HER TO ONE OF JIM'S FARMS.
I HEARD THEM TALKING ABOUT IT!

WHERE?! WHERE IS SHE?!

I WANT A LAWYER. I WANT PROTECTION AND I'LL TELL YOU.
I DIDN'T WANT TO KILL HIM.

I PROMISE YOU WON'T GET IN TROUBLE.
I SAW THE WHOLE THING, BUT IF YOU KNOW ABOUT A POSSIBLE KIDNAPPING?
YOU NEED TO TELL US WHERE SO WE CAN HELP THIS LITTLE GIRL.

YOU'RE RIGHT, I'M BEING SO SELFISH...OFF THE 270, WEST OF THE AIRPORT. WHERE HE'D DO ALL HIS POLITICAL RALLIES.
POLICE

THIS IS LIEUTENANT HOGAN, WE HAVE A POSSIBLE KIDNAPPING OF A MINOR BEING HELD AT THE PIG FARM OFF 270. PLEASE HAVE SWAT AND EVERYONE BE READY TO MOVE OUT IN FIVE.
LET'S GO!
YOU STAY WITH HER, TAKE HER TO THE HOSPITAL.
NO! NO! DON'T BELIEVE HER!
SHE AND BYRON SET THIS UP.
IT WAS THEM! THEY KILLED MY WIFE!
AHH! MY CHEST.
BDOM BDOM BDOM BDOM BDOM BDOM

BYRON... PLEASE! I'M REALLY HURT! I NEED A DOCTOR.
YOU GUYS, COME ON! WE NEED TO GO!
PALMER! WE'RE GOIN' AFTER YOUR DAUGHTER!
WHAT'S HAPPENING TO HIM?
I CAN'T FEEL MY ARM!
HE'S HAVING A HEART ATTACK.
JUST CALM DOWN AND TRY TO BREATH.
WE HAVE AN AMBULANCE ON STANDBY.
DON'T TOUCH ME! I SHOULD NEVER HAVE BELIEVED YOU!
IT'S YOU. YOU'RE THE BOAR.

HUMANS HAVE "THEORY OF MIND."
THEY CAN IMAGINE THE THOUGHTS AND FEELINGS OF OTHER PEOPLE. PIGS AREN'T THAT DIFFERENT.
SOME PEOPLE FIND IT DISGUSTING THAT A PIG WILL EAT A HUMAN BODY.
I THINK IT'S BEAUTIFUL.
THEY ARE, AFTER ALL, THE MOST SIMILAR CREATURES TO US OTHER THAN THE CHIMPANZEE.
EMERGENCY
POLICE
SWAT
BE CAREFUL.
IT MAY BE BOOBY TRAPPED.
DEATH TO PIGS

THIS MAN KILLED YOUR MOTHER. DON'T YOU WANT TO SEE HIM DIE?
OPEN THEM!
I SAID OPEN THEM OR WE FEED YOU TO THE PIGS NEXT.
HE WAS OUR LEADER...
shake
BUT HE BETRAYED US. SO NOW HE DIES TOO.
GRANDPA!
NOOOOOOO!!!!...

CRAP! WE NEED TO GET THIS OPEN!
WE'LL NEED GRINDING EQUIPMENT TO GET THROUGH THESE LOCKS.
NO TIME!
WE MAY ALREADY BE TOO LATE...
...I'VE GOT A BETTER IDEA.
POLICE
POLICE

VROOOM VROOOM
YOU HEAR THAT?!
OH, FUCK!

WHITE
LIONS
463

3
BIO-WASTE
466

HELP!

HELP!
HELP!
ARE THERE ANY MORE?
I DON'T KNOW.
I JUST WANT MY DAD!
DAD!!
WHERE'S MY DADDY?!

YOU HAVE TO LISTEN TO ME...ALEXANDER BYRON KILLED MY WIFE.
YOU CAN'T LET HIM GET AWAY WITH IT.
I HAVEN'T BEEN A GOOD FATHER!
I PROMISED KAIA I WOULDN'T LEAVE HER!
I PROMISED!
ALER

CLEAR
CLEAR

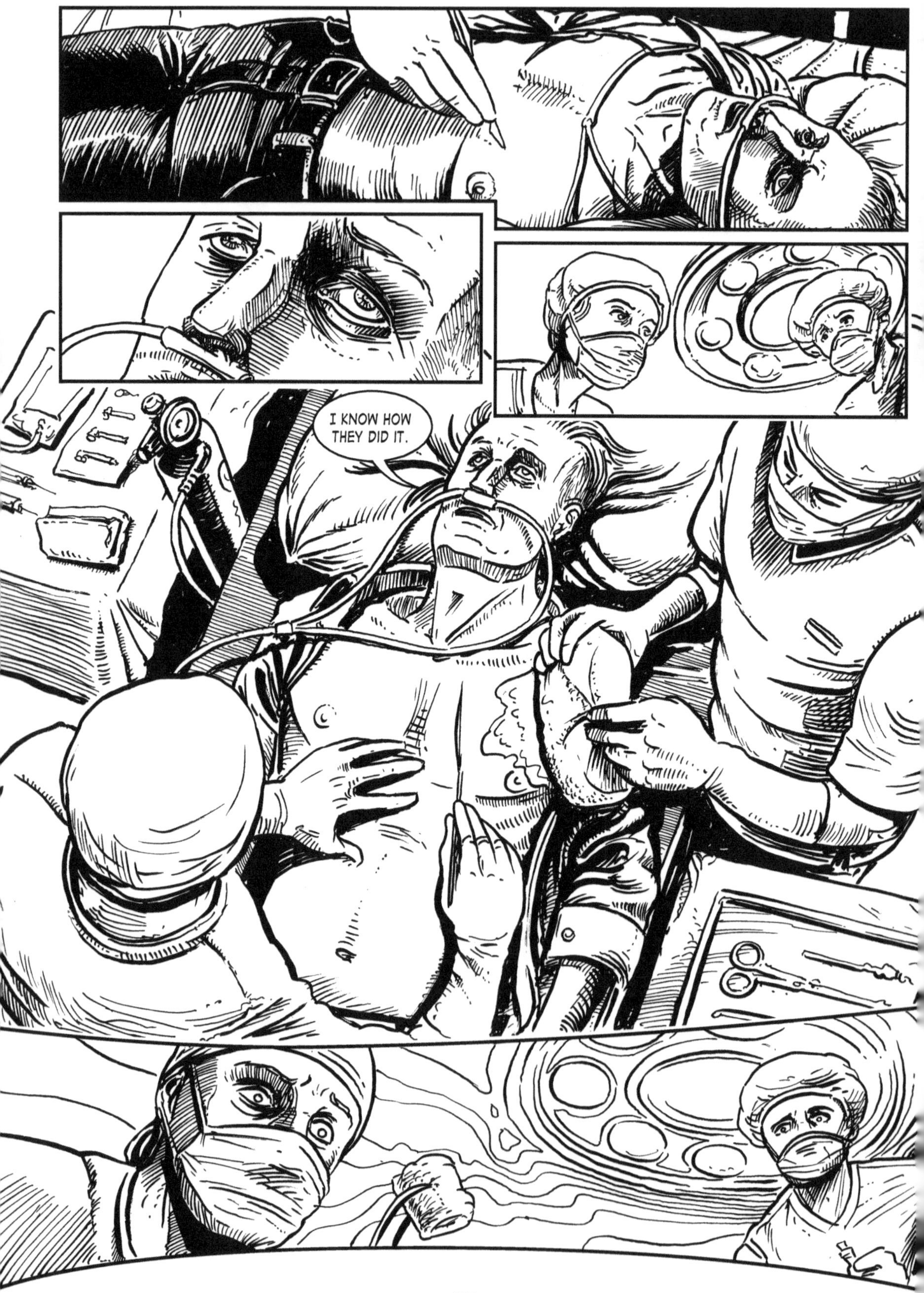
I KNOW HOW
THEY DID IT.

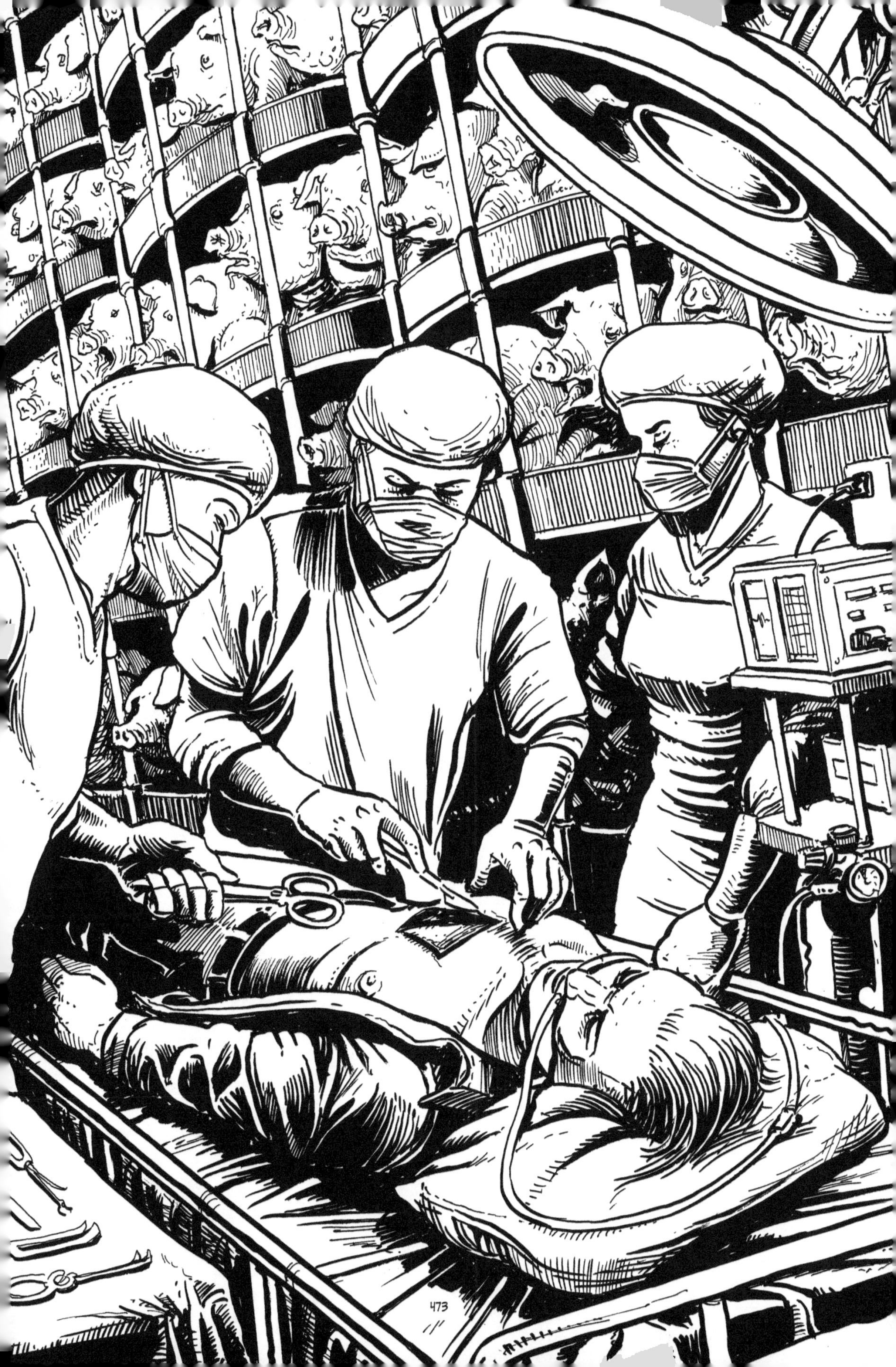
473

ORGAN ST

TEN YEARS EARLIER
SIT AND BE QUIET UNTIL YOUR HUSBAND GETS HERE.

HE'S WITH MY MOM!
BULLSHIT! HE LEFT WORK AN HOUR AGO.

WHAT IF SHE'S TELLING THE TRUTH?!

I AM!
HE'S NOT HERE!
HE'S IN LITTLE ROCK.

BAM
BA
BAM

WHAT THE FUCK, COLBA?
WHY WOULD YOU DO THAT?!
GOD DAMN IT, COLBA!

THE STUPID BITCH WAS LYING TO US.
THIS IS SO BAD!

HAVE YOU ANY IDEA HOW MUCH MORE COMPLICATED THIS IS NOW?

SHE'S DEAD...

ALRIGHT, ALRIGHT! I FUCKED UP...
WHAT ARE WE GONNA DO?

WE CALL LO.

FUCK!

PINK
GOAT

EXIT

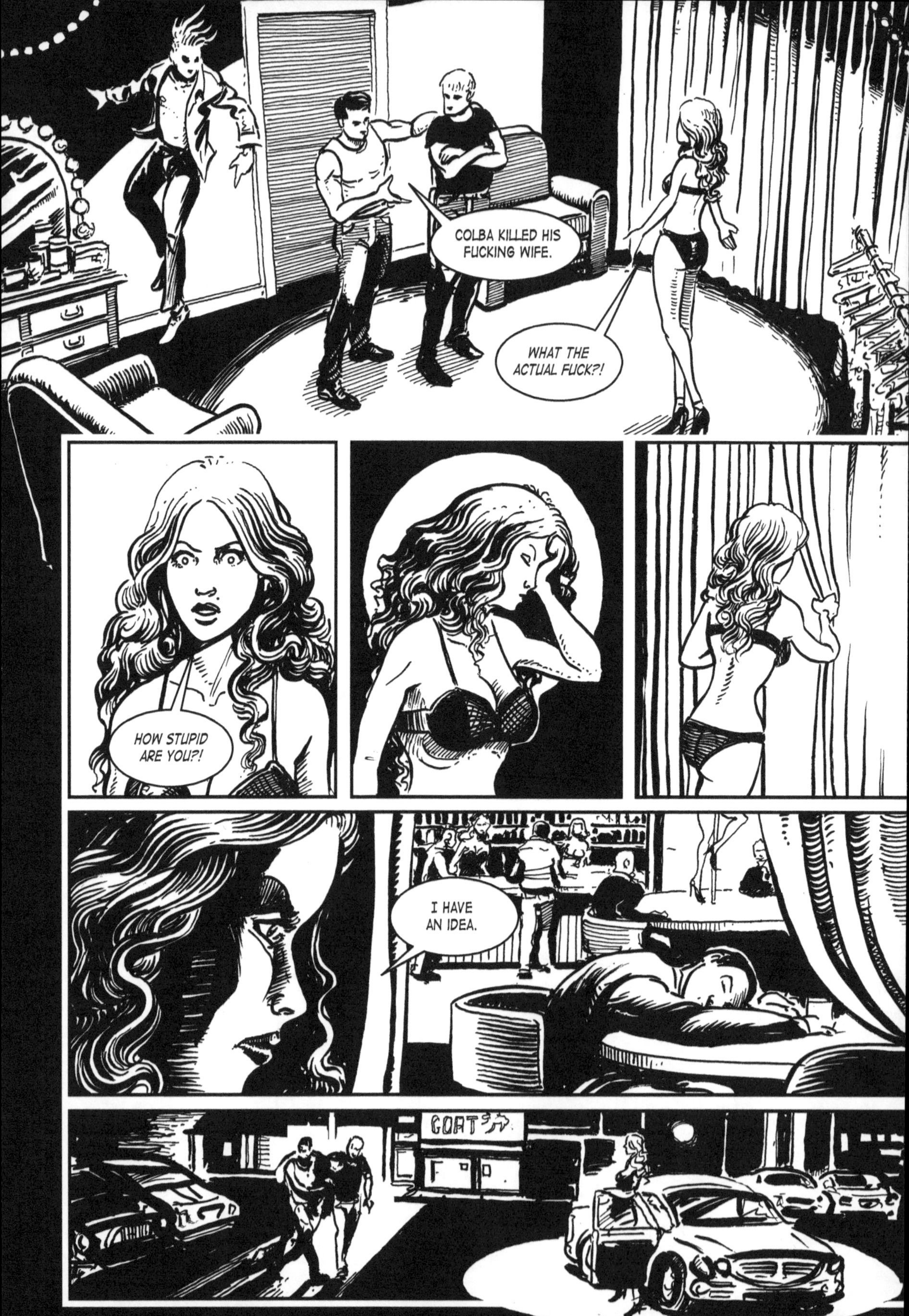

COLBA KILLED HIS FUCKING WIFE.

WHAT THE ACTUAL FUCK?!

BAM
BAM
BAM

HE'S BACK
HURRY! QUICK!

KAIA, WHAT'S WRONG?
I HEARD FIREWORKS!

FIREWORKS?

WHAT IS THAT?

IT'S HER DRESS. GET RID OF IT.

WHOOSH
484

BDOM
BDOM

BDOM
BDOM
BDOM
BDOM
BDOM
BDOM

THREE DAYS LATER...
DAD! YOU'RE AWAKE!
YOU'RE GOING TO HAVE TO WAIT UNTIL THEY CAN FIND A PROPER DONOR...
BUT THE DOCTORS SAID THE PIG HEART WOULD HAVE TO DO FOR NOW.
IT SAVED YOUR LIFE.

Hot Springs criminal ... man charged over a ... last ...

detectives raided a large estate at Hot Springs and two industrial sites in late August.

The 37-year-old will face court ... searched two homes ... industrial ...

They alleged ... kgs of cocaine and seven ... including an assault rifle, a Smith & Wesson revolver and semi-automatic pistols - hidden in a fake air conditioning unit above an apartment in Rockdale.

A search of the basement uncovered a further one kilogram of cocaine, one kilogram of ice, bulletproof vests, four firearms and ammunition.

The raids in Hot Springs turned up 25 litres of GBL, a drug commonly known as "coma in a bottle".

A 27-year-old man who was arrested and charged at the time remains before the courts.

... and man was arrested at a ... Hot Srings ...

on Friday morning.

They were charged with 25 offences, including two counts of supplying a large commercial quantity of prohibited drugs, an offence that carries a maximum penalty of life imprisonment.

They were also charged with seven counts of possessing an unauthorised prohibited firearm, possessing an unregistered firearm and not keeping a firearm safety-prohibited. The firearms are undergoing forensic and ballistic examination.

The alleged offenders were refused bail to face Hot Springs Bail Court on Saturday.

YOU CAN CALL ME, KAIA, DAD. I WANT YOU TO.
I SHOULD HAVE LISTENED TO YOU.
ARE THEY REALLY GOING TO GET AWAY WITH IT?...
WHAT KIND OF WORLD DO WE LIVE IN?
I DON'T KNOW. BUT I PROMISE YOU. I'LL NEVER LEAVE YOU AGAIN.

LATER THAT MONTH...

DRINK, MISS?
TEQUILA AND LIME, A SPLASH OF SODA WATER.

TO WIVES AND SWEETHEARTS, MAY THEY NEVER MEET.
CHINK

WHERE THE HELL IS THE STAFF?
I GAVE THEM THE NIGHT OFF.
WHY WOULD YOU DO THAT?
FOR US, BABE.

I...I...
...WHAT'S HAPPENING TO ME?
YOU...
...YOU COULDN'T.

THIS ISN'T GOING TO BE YOUR ARGENTINA, LO.
BUT...BUT....
I NEVER WANTED TO KILL ANYONE.
... I NEVER WOULD HAVE, IF I NEVER MET YOU.
495

POLIS
SCREE

BANG
BANG
BANG
BANG
BANG
BANG
BANG
...ARE WE PUNISHED FOR OUR SINS?

... OR DO OUR
SINS PUNISH US?

CHAPTER ELEVEN

Gone Fishin'

Dear Kaia,

I am overwhelmed with the joy that I am going to be a Grandpa.

You and Brandon are going to be the best parents in the world. It took me a while to explain but Nana understands she is going to be a Great Grandma!

We plan on moving out of the city soon. A cabin on the lake is something she has always wanted.

I love you,

Love,

Dad

NINE YEARS LATER
KNOCK KNOCK

AL PALMER'S $17M
SETTLEMENT
AGAINST STATE

Sooner or later we all get what we deserve

GRANDPA, HOW DO I DO IT?
plop

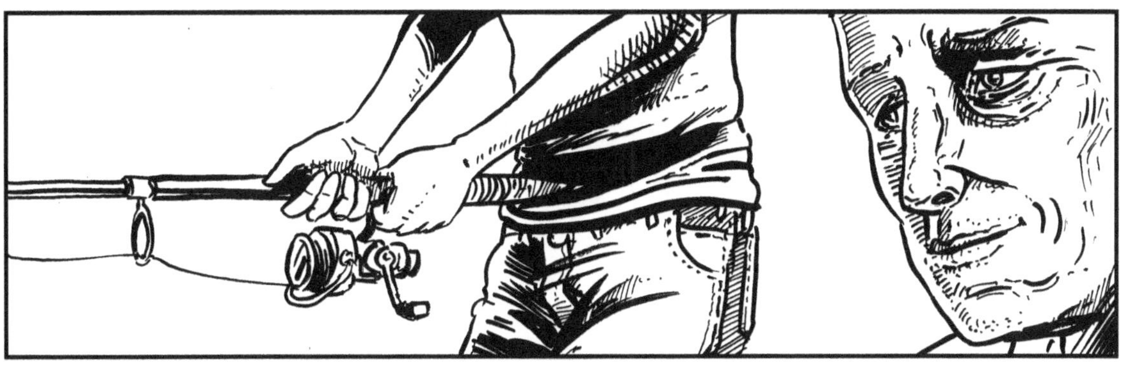

ROW, ROW, ROW YOUR BOAT, GENTLY DOWN THE STREAM....

MERRILY, MERRILY, MERRILY, MERRILY...

LIFE IS BUT
A DREAM.

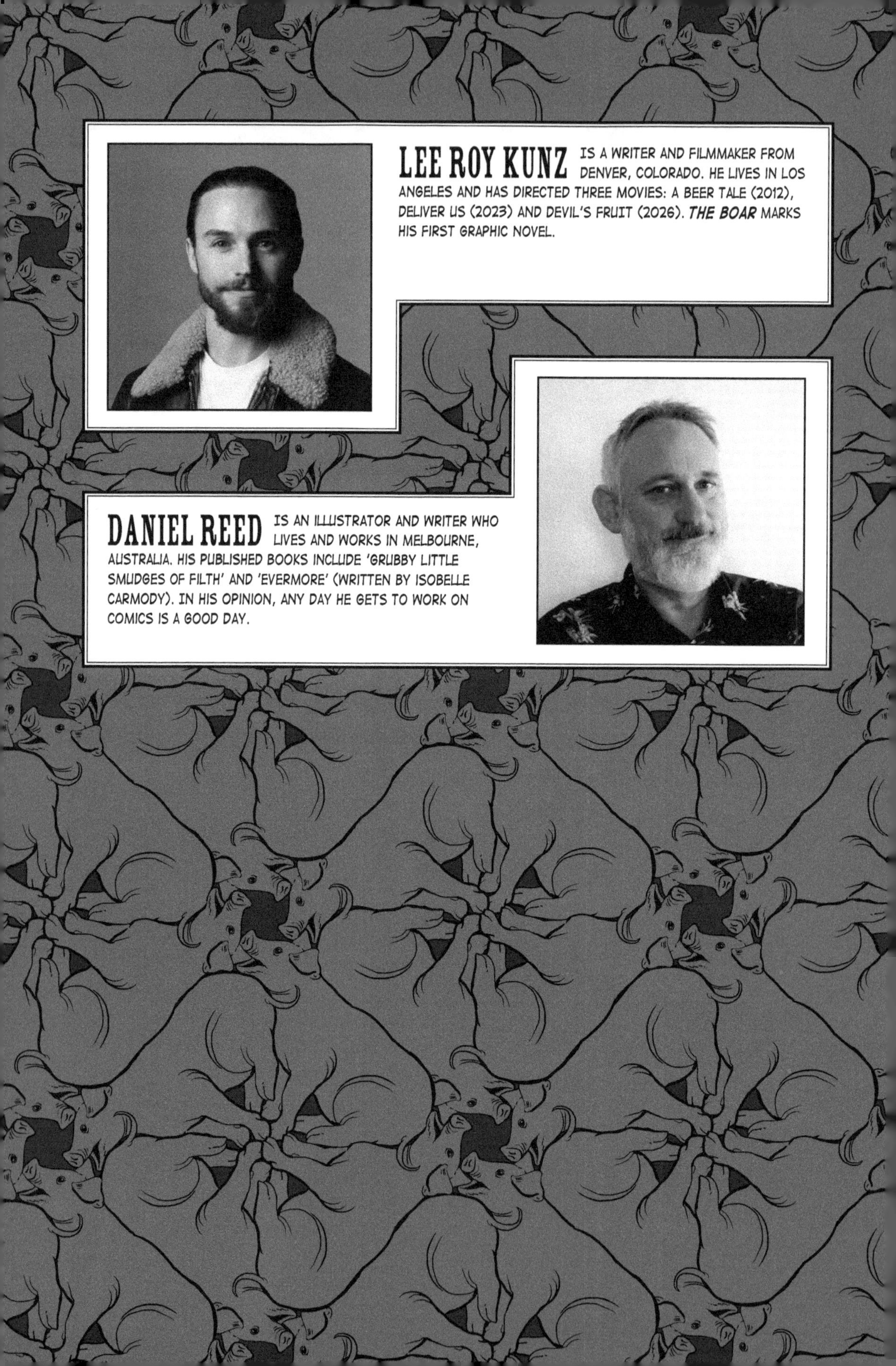

LEE ROY KUNZ IS A WRITER AND FILMMAKER FROM DENVER, COLORADO. HE LIVES IN LOS ANGELES AND HAS DIRECTED THREE MOVIES: A BEER TALE (2012), DELIVER US (2023) AND DEVIL'S FRUIT (2026). THE BOAR MARKS HIS FIRST GRAPHIC NOVEL.

DANIEL REED IS AN ILLUSTRATOR AND WRITER WHO LIVES AND WORKS IN MELBOURNE, AUSTRALIA. HIS PUBLISHED BOOKS INCLUDE 'GRUBBY LITTLE SMUDGES OF FILTH' AND 'EVERMORE' (WRITTEN BY ISOBELLE CARMODY). IN HIS OPINION, ANY DAY HE GETS TO WORK ON COMICS IS A GOOD DAY.